AMERICAN GIRL

a novel

Page Edwards Jr

Page Edwards

To Claudia,
It was good to have
you here in Cape May
Oct 14, 1991
Page

Marion Boyars

New York · London

Published in Great Britain and the United States
in 1990 by Marion Boyars Publishers
26 East 33rd Street, New York, NY 10016

Distributed in the United States and Canada by
Rizzoli International Publications Inc, New York

Distributed in Australia by
Wild and Woolley Pty Ltd, Glebe, NSW

Library of Congress Cataloging in Publication Data
Edwards, Page.
        American girl : a novel / Page Edwards.
        I. Title.
    PS3555.D95A8   1990
    813'.54—dc20   90–32607
                                                                         CIP

British Library Cataloguing in Publication Data
Edwards, Page, *1941*–
    American girl.
    I. Title
    813.54 [F]

ISBN 0–71145–2912–5   Cloth

Printed in Great Britain

AMERICAN
GIRL

for Benjamin Carter Edwards and Don Hendrie, Jr.

author's note

This is a work of fiction, although the character of Nancy Meade's grandmother Leellen-Kaye is based upon Louella Day McConnell, founder of the present-day Fountain of Youth in St. Augustine, Florida. Otherwise, any resemblance to any actual person living or dead is unintentional. Where the names of actual places are used, the situations and descriptions concerning those places are entirely fictional.

I would like to acknowledge the assistance and encouragement of the trustees and staff of the St. Augustine (Florida) Historical Society whose extensive library and archives I used to research the book, and of my friends Patricia Griffin, Howard Greenfeld, Ron Hansen and Rima Robbins.

Also, I express here my gratitude to those who have read early versions of *American Girl* and have offered advice as the work developed: namely, my love and thanks to my wife Diana; to my daughter Amy; and to my editor and publisher Marion Boyars.

Page Edwards Jr.
St. Augustine, Florida

PART 1

chapter 1
prologue

Nancy Meade's grandmother, Leellen-Kaye Phillips, was a portrait of health and independence when she came to St Augustine in August, 1902, on the Florida East Coast Special. As such she was rather a threat to us slow and more lugubrious southerners whom she found occupying her newly adopted city.

Frontier politics are unheard of here; we have lived next door to one another for generations. Law and order — and the corruption that goes along with it — and family are what matter here.

We are entrenched, and Leellen-Kaye never thoroughly understood that, and neither did her daughter-in-law, Ben's wife Kaye-Ann. If Nancy's grandmother fled the Yukon because of corrupt officials, as she claimed she did, she was no doubt surprised to discover that she had moved into a world equally corrupt and mean, one which in the end would wear down her grace and rare beauty as fast as any frontier. In any event, it is amazing that she lived to be eighty, and that her daughter-in-law waited as long as she did to kill herself. It may be too soon to tell if the same thing that happened to Leellen-Kaye and to Ben's wife will also happen to Ben's daughter Nancy, but if she isn't watchful no doubt the identical wedge which parted Nancy's grandmother from reality will do the same to her.

On that afternoon in August, 1902, half the city turned out for a look at Mr and Mrs Sidney Phillips who were supposed to be very rich and elegant from selling their gold mines, having left the Yukon Territory two months earlier travelling by skiff from Dawson and boat to Fairbanks, Nome and San Francisco, then by the Southern Pacific Railway to change in Jacksonville for Henry Morrison Flagler's private car to St Augustine. Her husband — reputed to be the laziest man the Klondike had ever seen — carried away from the gold fields a tobacco tin full of nuggets (ca. $75,000); Leellen-Kaye had $40,000 sewn in her skirt hem — proceeds from the sale of her Melbourne Hotel in Dawson — and wore a nugget bracelet and diamond necklace with a stone missing. In Dawson she had hired a dentist for $600 to remove one of the stones and use it to fill a cavity in her front tooth instead of common gold. They booked a suite at the Ponce de Leon Hotel, took tea at the Alcazar across King Street and steamed away the travel aches in their bones in the Casino baths above the indoor pool at the rear of the hotel.

The couple stayed at the Ponce de Leon but after a month they purchased an appropriate house, a large white Carpenter Gothic, in the middle of an orange grove off the Shell Road on Magnolia Avenue in North City, for $14,000. A beautiful palmetto–shaded drive gave entrance to the house, bordered by large oleanders. Peach and cedar trees spotted the orange grove, the evergreens providing an umbrella from winter frost. Elaborate rose gardens and shrub-lined walks surrounded the house (which Leellen-Kaye later disassembled and rebuilt on Water Street where it stands today as Phillips House). Most significant was the hand-dug well on the property, a tidal pool of brackish water which would in 1906 become the Fountain of Youth, the legendary object of Ponce de Leon's search in

1513 and the sole invention of Leellen-Kaye Phillips. Though Leellen-Kaye lived to be eighty and called St Augustine her true and only home, she was born in Hills, Iowa, in 1875 and studied medicine at the state university, becoming one of the first female physicians in the country. In 1898 (she was twenty-three) she took her medical practice to the Yukon Territory where she met her husband, whom she described as a tall Adonis with broad shoulders and black black hair, strong as a bull. Of course, Leellen-Kaye herself was striking, strong as a man yet with beautiful features and blond hair she pinned up in a style well ahead of its time. Life was hard those four years in the Klondike — a place where scurvy was prevalent, as were temperatures fifty degrees below zero, morphine, avalanches, cheap liquor, dance halls and gambling rooms. If she, in 1895, was tenacious as the single female medical student in Iowa City, then the gold camps only made her more so.

When they arrived on the Special that afternoon, everyone waited to catch a glimpse of Mrs Phillips' smile, to see for themselves the diamond flash, and to admire her ermine coat. Later the gentlemen played billiards and discussed where the Phillipses might install themselves. The William Loomis property in North City was a good buy since the last winter's freeze had killed two-thirds of his oranges. Sidney paid cash for the place the next afternoon while Leellen-Kaye had tea in the Grand Parlor; she wore a ring with jewels on every finger of both hands, including her thumbs, and her white fur coat touched the floor.

The entire town talked of their immense wealth as they replanted the garden with roses and built an aviary for the Mongolian pheasants which they brought in from Spokane and filled the Loomis house with furniture sent down from New York and Philadelphia on the Atlantic Seaboard Line. Most often Sidney Phillips was away on business (in the Klondike supposedly) and Leellen kept a room in the Ponce de Leon for nights when she was too exhausted to take a

carriage alone to her house in North City. At one point Sidney
Phillips was gone for six months. He came back and a month
later took her away with him. This was in winter, about 1904.
Nothing was heard of them, but we assumed they had
returned to the Klondike to care for their mining interests.

They left the house and two large dogs (a Newfoundland
and a St Bernard) with their caretaker George Manucy.
Spring came and George still had no word from them. Early
that summer both the dogs became infested with fleas and
someone suggested to George that he trim their coats. George
did just that: he and his wife got drunk and shaved them both
to the skin. With the fur gone, they were the sorriest looking
creatures you have ever seen and, according to George
Manucy so funny looking that he had either to turn them loose
in the country or else his wife was going to laugh herself to
death. Even with her dogs gone, Leellen-Kaye kept George on
as caretaker until he died in 1948.

Sidney and Leellen-Kaye were gone more than two years.
Then she came back alone on the night train and walked from
the station to North City because she was broke. George saw
her coming and thought at first she was a vagrant, a snow
bird. She still had her jewelry and her coat and would not sell
them. She had no clothes and put together a wardrobe out of
the living room curtains and began to call the well on her
place the Fountain of Youth. Her old friends rode out to
welcome her home, and she tried to sell them the water for
fifty cents a glass. Not many bought, so she fenced it in, had
George Manucy put up a shrine over the well, and began to
collect admission to her property. This was in 1906, a time
when we had fewer winter visitors down here from the north
staying in the three big Flagler hotels, a time when we all did
what we could to stop the tourist flow to the newer hotels at
Palm Beach and Coconut Grove. Leellen-Kaye with her
Fountain of Youth attracted her share. George built a gambling pavilion out at her place; she hired some women to stay
out there, and traffic on the Shell Road to North City got

steady. A few years later, Sidney Phillips showed up to make Leellen-Kaye pregnant with twins before he left again. The report was that he had lost all his money and had to go back alone to Dawson and get some more.

Leellen-Kaye was thirty-seven when she had the twins. The day they were born she decided she could never afford to send both of them off to school, so she flipped a coin: Jack would stay with her and run the Fountain of Youth; Ben would become a doctor like her. As soon as Jack could walk he was selling water with his mother. When he heard a carriage coming, he ran to the gate to coax it into the Fountain of Youth. Leellen-Kaye dressed her boy to look like a pint-sized businessman with hat and cane. You must understand that she was no longer a poor woman with no source of income begging at passers-by and wearing a dress made from the living room curtains. She had a thriving business: a whore house with class, a gambling pavilion, a tourist attraction of international renown which the poor as well as the rich people from up north had heard of and wanted to see for themselves. Leellen-Kaye was making a fortune out at her place, marketing quick money, eternal youth and love (sex). Leellen-Kaye's was the hottest in town and cleaner than the houses in West Augustine or Little Africa where George Manucy's wife worked. On the pretext of visiting the true and authentic landing spot of Don Juan Ponce de Leon in 1513, Grover Cleveland came and so did Presidents Arthur and Billy Sunday, who claimed to drink fifteen glasses of 'youth juice' offered by fifteen different Indian Maidens in 1921. Theodore Draper was repulsed by the place on Christmas Day in 1925 and wrote in his diary that the woman who ran the Fountain of Youth was not only crazy, but also old.

In fact, Leellen-Kaye Phillips was not yet fifty in 1925, and her boys were thirteen. Ben came home from boarding school in the north that Christmas; and the photographer E.A.

Meyers made a portrait of Leellen-Kaye posed with her sons in front of the fountain.

She looks regal in that photograph, if somewhat dazed (she had developed a cocaine habit by that time). The boys are almost miniatures of what they would be at sixty: Ben, the Southern Gentleman; Jack, the glassy-eyed huckster with a stoop. Their mother is standing between them looking almost the lady, but there remains upon her face some of the weathered look of a woman who has run her own business on some frontier or other. There is one person missing from that Christmas 1925 portrait: Sidney Phillips, the father, who is supposed to be dead, but who is in fact working for Paramount as a technical adviser on gold rush films and living on Orange Street in Hollywood, California, behind the jungle set which resembles the Florida swamp upon which the company filmed monster, horror and animal movies like Tarzan before sound. Sidney Phillips, who only dreamed of making his second fortune on the silver screen, is missing. Leellen-Kaye is forty-nine. She is the woman who her husband said was crazy, but she has made her second fortune by this time, selling youth and promoting love.

She would have no more children than these two; the set of wan and pale twins satisfied her. However, there was a child who would enter the portrait a few years later, Kaye-Ann Manucy, George the caretaker's daughter. She was a year old at the time of the portrait and white as George was, living with her dusty-brown mother in Little Africa. She would come to live at the Fountain of Youth immediately after her mother's death to cook for Leellen-Kaye and keep house and help her father and Jack when she could, raking the oyster shell paths in the garden, straining the scum and dead insects off the water in the fountain, collecting whiskey bottles and trash outside the gambling pavilion, the jetsam of the life that went on inside at night. She was a sweet girl, Kaye-Ann was, obedient and guilt-free. She began accommodating Jack in the empty pavilion when she was fourteen, and it is a wonder she didn't get pregnant before she did, supposedly by Ben. During the day Kaye-Ann dressed as an Indian Maiden and told visitors the story of Ponce de Leon and afterwards served them water from the Fountain. That was about the time that Leellen-Kaye determined that this was not the best place in which to raise children, so she disassembled the house and had it moved to Water Street where it stands today in the heart of the Abbott Tract overlooking Hospital Creek, the Matanzas River and out past the inlet to the Atlantic Ocean.

Leellen-Kaye had about a dozen girls working for her then. They lived at the Fountain under the protection of old George. Most of the girls were homeless, abandoned, orphaned, or pregnant: Leellen-Kaye's place looked like a school for wayward girls most mornings, with two or three of them in the garden, a couple more hanging out the wash, a few more raking the oyster shell paths and picking up papers and trash and bottles. What schooling these girls got was from Leellen-Kaye herself. She taught them about Don Juan Ponce de Leon, about eternal youth as a commodity, about advertising and men (not the hows of sexual intercourse, but the coquettish ploys: 'Use your eyes first,' she taught them, 'then your hands, and only last use your mouth. You will find in the short run this will be sufficient. Remember that most of our visitors are just that, they are simply passing through. You will probably never see them again in your lives. Above all, don't fall in love.')

After Ben finished prep school and entered Dartmouth College, Jack began running the Fountain from noon to five, after which his mother took over for the evening trade. By the time Ben had dropped out of medical school and was on a tour of the continent, Jack had taken over management of the Fountain of Youth and runs it today (just within the law) as his mother ran it before him. The gambling is gone and the girls no longer live in a house on the property and solicit openly, but the Indian Maidens are still there, telling the same story that they have told for more than seventy years.

Jack has lived in the old whorehouse at the Fountain with three wives, driving each one of them away after a year or so. At sixty-three he still prefers the young and pliant ones and seems to be happily resigned to helping himself to his willing Indian Maidens when the need strikes, rather than growing old with a wife. Though Jack will never admit to it in this life, some of us believe that he never loved George Manucy's daughter the way he said he did, but that along with the 'broken heart' that Kaye-Ann gave him — she also gave him a lifelong excuse to womanize.

She moved to the Fountain when she was eleven. Though she knew Jack far better, Ben was always the mysterious one to Kaye-Ann, because he was away at school most of the time. So no matter how the intimacy between Jack and Kaye-Ann progressed from eyes, then to hands, and then to mouths, it was finally Ben whom Kaye-Ann declared to be the father of her child, which seemed reasonable since Ben and Kaye-Ann were inseparable, and Jack at that time already had his second wife, Marylin Joe Sabate, a juicy little Minorcan bean of a woman who had been one of Jack's Indian Maidens since high school.

Nancy, Kaye-Ann's daughter, was born eight months after Kaye-Ann and Ben were married, and both of them were devoted to the child. When Kaye-Ann got sick, if anyone held that marriage together, it was that little girl Nancy who later married her professor boyfriend because she was pregnant just like her mother had been, but who is much too much like Leellen-Kaye, too strange and unpredictable, to make her own marriage hold together. That's probably because the little girl lived in a house dominated first by the grandmother, then by a mother who maintained various aspects of the grandmother after the old lady died in that freak car wreck on Anastasia Island in 1955. The papers got two extras out of that wreck, mainly because of who the old lady was — the inventor of the most profitable tourist attraction in North Florida — and how they found her body nothing but a heap of red dress with the jewelry gone and the diamond in her tooth missing, and her mouth stuffed full of sand, looking for all the world like she had been run off the road, strangled and robbed. Sidney Phillips, the failed movie mogul, arrived in town from Hollywood, California, to try and break the will, declaring the 1912 divorce null and void, but Jack's lawyer Leo Pacetti out-danced the old man's, and Ben and Jack gave their father an annuity and sent him back to the west coast. We heard that he died, this time for certain, in the early sixties.

No one in this town is going to forget Nancy Meade's grandmother, Leellen-Kaye Phillips. Though she was never properly thanked for it, she was one of the business people who pulled us out of an economic slump after Henry Flagler moved his hotel business further south to Palm Beach and Coconut Grove and Miami. Nothing short of a startling attraction like the Fountain of Youth would pull the sun-starved tourists from the north off the southbound trains for a visit here. We all know that there is no such item as the Fountain of Youth. It is a complete fantasy, but fantasy sells in Florida, and Jack Phillips knows how to market it. He markets it better than the old lady did herself, because she started believing in the place and had to take her cocaine to effect the renewal the fantasy promised. So what if Jack's cocaine is girls in their twenties. He believes young girls keep him young, and maybe they do. We all admit that Jack is a prime case, of arrested development to the point that he continues to act like a twenty year-old at sixty-three, but there's your eternal youth for you, in person. Jack is as Jack is and always will be. He is loyal to his young women and to that youth juice they pass out to the tourists. He has been trading on that myth for fifty years and is a rich man because of it. And he has made his brother Ben a rich man, too, and never complained about it. Both those brothers are set up for life from selling nothing but water with a story attached to it. Now, that's an all-American success story. It begins with a vain woman who has two boys to raise herself; she strikes it rich because people buy her story that she discovered the true Fountain of Youth. There is no one who won't give up a few dollars for a taste of a myth. And the reason we respect Jack Phillips as much as we do is because he has never carried the business any further than giving people what they want: a good show.

If you carry it beyond that the trouble begins. That's how Leellen-Kaye and Kaye-Ann, after her, got themselves in trouble. The truth began to blur. Old Leellen-Kaye came to believe the water actually did something for her and set about trying to convince people that her Fountain was not something she had made up to keep from starving after she went broke the first time. The imaginary served as a wedge which separated her from the rest of us. Once she began to believe the fantasy she had created, she was gone from us, separated. The only one she took with her when she left was Ben's wife, Kaye-Ann.

The success of her fantasy was so great that she set about trying to prove something was true that wasn't ever true, and both she and Kaye-Ann wound up as paranoid as whipped cats. It would put a man on dope or drink if he set about trying to prove that a lie he started, and everyone else played along with, was actually the truth. Why couldn't the old lady just be thankful for the dollars from the happy tourists and let it go at that? No, the more money the place made, the more she wanted that well of hers to be real. She wouldn't listen to you when you told her in a calm, reasonable manner that there is or never was such a thing to begin with. She had developed an obsession to make right by an old lie, and that did Leellen-Kaye Phillips in, and she passed her obsession on, not to Jack, not to Ben, but to her daughter-in-law Kaye-Ann who killed herself with bourbon and 'youth juice'; and neither Ben nor their daughter Nancy could do a damn thing to help Kaye-Ann but stay close to her and love her as best they knew how.

At one point, Leellen-Kaye, who was almost eighty by this time, persuaded Ben to send Kaye-Ann to Spain. Leellen-Kaye wanted some historical ammunition to support her claim. Ben hoped that research in the Archives of the Indies would reveal the truth to his wife and get the bug out of her. But Kaye-Ann brought back records, copies of hundreds of them, which she said proved conclusively that Ponce de Leon had landed in the exact spot on Florida's eastern coast where the lie claimed he did. Then an old red cedar blew down on the property, and she got money from Ben to pay a couple of workmen to be quiet about laying out a cross with fifteen stones going one way and thirteen the other. Under one of the stones she set a silver cup and a photocopied document written by Ponce de Leon. So Jack and Ben took her to find out the truth from the librarian of the local historical society. They had stacks of documents with them. Miss Kirby went over each one telling her what each one of them was and how it related to their property. The Spanish documents were about Ponce's discovery of Florida, his life in Puerto Rico, his contract to explore Bimini, his death and his monument in Havana harbor. When she finished Kaye-Ann's documents, Miss Kirby told her that they did not relate in any way to their property or to the well Leellen-Kaye Phillips had 'found' in 1906, but to the whole of Florida, Puerto Rico, Cuba, and the islands off Key West. Jack and Ben and Kaye-Ann had asked Miss Kirby to tell them the truth. She told them that the Fountain of Youth was a dug well, the cross was fake, and that the water in the well rose and dropped because it was partially fed by the ocean which is why it tastes brackish. Kaye-Ann lost her temper and refused to believe Miss Kirby was telling the truth.

They took the real estate documents to Miss Kirby who examined the chain of title. Jack told her that he wanted to publish a little booklet that would give the true story of the place, so Miss Kirby wrote a statement and took it to the family and read it aloud to them. She told Ben and Jack and

Kaye-Ann that she would let him publish her statement only if they would abolish Kaye-Ann's false cross, fill in the dug well, and stop telling the tourists stories that had been invented by their mother. All three of them refused.

Ben and Jack realized immediately that Miss Kirby was asking them to put a tourniquet on their income. Kaye-Ann believed that Miss Kirby was intent on discrediting the family, that she was lying to them, so Kaye-Ann swore she would prove that Ponce de Leon did land where Leellen-Kay Phillips said he did, and that he did set down the stone cross and leave the silver cup and the document behind to show that he was there, and she swore she would prove that the well on their property was not a hand-dug well but was a spring, the Fountain of Eternal Youth as discovered in 1513 by Don Juan Ponce de Leon himself. She told Miss Kirby in so many words what she could do with her true history of the two hundred and fifty acres in North City owned by the Phillips family. Later Kaye-Ann tried to buy it from her, probably to burn it, but Miss Kirby wouldn't sell. Next she tried to buy Miss Kirby's silence and was refused. So Kaye-Ann went to the president of the local historical society and made a large donation, more than enough to build the society the new library it needed. The string attached to the gift was that if any employee of the society ever made discrediting statements against any historic site in town, his or her employment would be terminated. Miss Kirby kept her mouth shut, and her real truth of the Fountain of Youth was not found until many years later, buried in the stacks of notes she had made on various topics over her long years of service.

Kaye-Ann may have shamed her husband who loved her just about as much as any man could, and he never understood why she could not admit that she was exploiting people's fantasy, making their lives easier to bear, but he never let the wedge she drove between her world and the world around her cut into his heart. Instead his love became an umbrella for her, and underneath it Kaye-Ann continued trying to make people believe that the Fountain was just as real as the Egyptian chamberpot in the Metropolitan Museum and the 'Irises' by van Gogh. Ben's umbrella protected her for her whole life.

If the past is any test, the Phillips women, not the men, listen to the devil in the well. The men look after the pay–out. And if it hasn't happened already, Nancy Meade will listen to the same devil and go down the way her grandmother and her mother have gone down. Maybe it has happened to her already; no one here has seen much of her since her marriage busted up and she came home. Maybe she has already done something to herself that has wedged the real away from the imaginary inside of her, inside where the real and the imaginary are meant to be all jumbled up. If so, she will follow her kin and select the imaginary and live by those lights and we will not see her again, at least not as we used to know her.

We worry about Ben. He has had twenty years with a woman living by different lights. She shot a horse she caught drinking from the well and was arrested for discharging a firearm within the city limits. She hired a circus to mock the Fountain's power over her. The speculators got to her in private, and she signed papers for a race track. She did many queer things. She lobbied for free tolls on the Panama Canal claiming it would increase visitation at the well. She was arrested for having a German wireless on the property at the end of World War II, and for broadcasting advertisements about the Fountain to off-shore submarines. She claimed that one afternoon old Sheriff Pierce gave her an apple which made Capo's colt drop dead. She was talked about, mocked and considered as crazy as her mother-in-law was. And her drinking got so that she couldn't leave the house, so she used the telephone. Her dementia flowed into the ears of every influential resident, then it began to flow out of the instrument and onto the papers which the listener had abandoned on his desk without her knowing that she was talking to someone who had recognized her rasping slurring voice and had set down the receiver and gone to the can while she spoke on and on and on. She lived by different lights for twenty years and damn near killed Ben, who stood beside her, always blind with love for her. He detested his father for leaving his mother in the same condition and vowed not to do the same no matter how it got with Kaye-Ann. Finally she killed herself.

To make the death easier on his daughter, Ben told Nancy that her mother had died by mistake, that Dr Carver had prescribed Seconal to help her sleep, but the night she died she took too many by mistake. In fact, Ben admitted later, Kaye-Ann was addicted to the barbiturate and had tried to kick the drug too suddenly, which killed her. That night she had flushed all of her pills on impulse. When the convulsions and body twitchings began, she locked herself in the master bedroom down the hall from Nancy's room (Nancy was a senior in high school then) and tried to drink away the pain, too ashamed to call for help.

Ben took a tailspin after that and many of us didn't think he would recover. His daughter Nancy went off with that professor of hers, leaving him alone in the big house with the memories. He kept the living memory of Kaye-Ann with him, and for eight years he lived alone in that house of his. His daughter came to visit now and again (mainly to get away from her husband). But for all the rest of it he sat inside day after day. Then a few months ago he surprised us all by showing up on the golf course one Saturday with his brother like nothing had happened. He had a slice to the left, which he corrected; his putting lacked authority on the first nine, then evened out. He shot an eighty-three that day and beat Jack by two. Since then his handicap has dropped from seven to four.

Ben doesn't talk about those eight years he mourned for Kaye-Ann. But he must have put himself through some hell to come out of it the way he did; a little overweight, but clear-eyed, his faculties in better shape than any of us have ever seen before. And now he's got that striking blond lawyer (the Miller girl) for all the world crazy in love with him. There's no question but his daughter helped him some. She comes home often enough to work on her studies. Still you must hand it to Ben, give him applause and roses. Had it been any one of us, we would have gone dodging and ducking under the tragedy of it all and ended in a mess of booze and seafoam. Not Ben Phillips. He took himself straight through his shame and his grief, and he came out of it healed about as good as you can expect from any man.

But the sad part of it is that Ben used up so much love taking care of his mother and then his wife, that his daughter Nancy got sort of left out of it. She grew up almost by herself in a house full of eccentrics. She's got her studies; she's spent effort on that Sallie Stevens person she's writing about. Ben says that sometimes Nancy acts like that Sallie person is alive: it's all so real to her. Yes, it's the daughter with the broken marriage we wonder about.

She has been home since before Easter and no one has seen her out of the house. Nancy always was solitary, even as a child, but there are times when a person needs someone else, someone to talk to. There isn't a person in this world that doesn't need someone to talk to in a time of death or unhappiness, no one in this world, whether they'll admit to it or not.

chapter two

My name is Nancy Meade. I am twenty-six and have two boys — Tom is seven, and Alan is four. I have left my husband and, for now, live at home. I can't stay here forever, I realize that. But my father will allow me to stay long enough for me to make sense of what has happened to my life so far — so I don't fly dazed into the woods like a convalescing heron with a half-mended wing, the way I did after my mother died.

I am not free yet. I am not free to run and leap; possibly freedom is not the point anyway.

Months ago — maybe years ago — something went wrong and stayed that way. My happiness, or unhappiness for that matter, had virtually nothing to do with the quality of my life, which was good enough. I have always had my own money; the boys have always been healthy; my husband wasn't all that unfaithful, not by comparison with some professors. Some time ago I got in the habit of projecting and acting upon what I thought Arthur my husband wanted, not what I wanted. I knew perfectly well that to try and fulfill his wants was beyond my life and control, but I tried to do that anyway. It didn't work.

So I made myself try to live day to day in the present. I would not allow myself to project at all. I tried to stop the film.

Stop it if I could whenever I caught myself wishing for anything. It was at that time I began to feel cold, almost paralyzed, languid. I thought that what was wrong must lie somewhere in the realm of my spirit.

My life was safe, but not right. More often than not I had these dead sensations as if an unknown force was pushing me, waist deep, slowly through a swamp toward an indefinite goal. I was stuck, but in motion, as if I were not in control. Mechanical. Dead.

Physically, I was unrelentingly exhausted, slept deeply, but was awakened often by endless dreams. I stopped enjoying the companionship of my two boys. Something had gone bad in my heart: the surges of passion for my husband which had overwhelmed me even a year before, in spite of his other women, no longer swept over me. Although my life was stable for the most part, I didn't want what I had. It seemed meaningless. So I waited like a sniper for him to do something outrageous enough to give me an excuse to leave him; waited because I had nothing concrete, no truly plausible excuse to warrant my packing up the children and leaving him, because I lacked the courage.

Then one day the excuse came. And I was on the road. But freedom was not on my mind that afternoon when I packed the kids in the car and came home. I know the road. I should. I drove home on it at least once a month for almost eight years: four of college as a history major, then three of graduate school in sociology for my masters, then, finally, my last year when I switched to ethnology to begin that doctorate I'll never finish. I must have driven the road hundreds of times. But never in such an emotional state, never with the recklessness of one running toward instead of away. Freedom? It's certain I was not free that afternoon.

I remember the clear pavement ahead unrolling over the swamp, moving parallel with a stream for a time, then cutting back through a 'shack-and-dance hall' town. It was early spring. Time for the cabbage harvest. At one point, I lifted my foot from the accelerator to let a tractor I was trying to pass glide on ahead so I could drift back into my lane. Gripping the steering wheel, I got ready for the blast of air from an oncoming semi.

I was on the road at last. Then I pulled out to pass the slow green tractor, with a stake-bed trailer loaded with cabbages. It swerved half off the pavement, throwing puffs of dust, shaped like light brown melons which hung in the humid air. Past the swerving trailer, I glanced in the mirror. The old farmer yapped soundlessly at my almost getting both of us mowed down by the semi. I looked at myself. Eyes red. Mascara smeared.

A slow-moving bus full of children, lights flashing, finally stopped. I waited. Then came another tractor hauling a harvester on a flat-bed.

A field of cabbages, dense and lush, opened up to the left. Spaced along the roadside was a series of signs that called in swift succession, 'Carrots,' 'Pepper Sauce,' 'Okra,' 'Cabbages,' 'Sweet Onions.' The weathered vegetable stand went by. Then I passed an identical string of signs facing the other direction on the opposite side of the road. Reading the words in the mirror, I drifted across the double yellow line, marking time for an opening around a low white Cadillac with a driver whose bald head appeared to be nesting on the back of the seat. I moved up close, saw an opening, floored it, and squeezed by just before a station wagon shot past. The horns from both the Caddy and the wagon sounded as one and became deeper as I pulled away.

My oldest boy, Tom was thrilled with my bad driving. He was sitting next to me, imitating my steering, oblivious to the warnings and the danger. 'Blow your horn back at them, Mom!'

My younger son, Alan, was stretched across the back seat, asleep among snack wrappers and soda cans from another more placid excursion to Cypress Gardens a few weeks before. The luggage section was packed to the ceiling with loose clothing and shoes, an iron under Alan's feet, a blow-dryer on the floor. Bug-spattered boxes and suitcases were tied on the luggage rack with the clothes line which once ran from the trailer to the single live oak in our yard at the trailer court.

At the open gravel area where Route 16 turns east, sometimes a man and woman sell boiled peanuts from the trunk of a black Chrysler at the corner. I watched for them. And for the single old man in blue coveralls and the battered blue truck with racks of smoked mullet hanging like dried wings. That day a green awning was shading a mound of darker green.

I slowed for the turn. Off to the right, from behind a dense row of trees, a small airplane dropped in front of us and passed low over the bare field, leaving behind four ribbons of white that hung dead in the air. The engine sounded like my father's riding mower. 'What a noisy butterfly,' said Tom.

'What butterfly?' Alan piped up from the back seat. He always comes half awake when the car slows.

The little plane lifted and rotated above us and dropped out of sight beyond a windbreak of slash pine to dust another newly planted potato field. We passed the open gravel area. A lone woman, dressed in white, stood under the green awning. She was surrounded by cabbages.

No vehicle in sight — only the woman, sad-eyed, lost as if she had been dropped from the sky. She reminded me of Sallie. She seemed located somehow, not waiting. She was Sallie Stevens.

'Who's that?' asked sleepy Alan. 'I want Dixie.'

'That's Sallie,' I said.

'I want Dixie, too,' said Tom. 'He's my dog.'

'He's mine.'

'Hush, both of you! Your father has him, and that's that. Dixie will be fine. Besides, there isn't enough room in the car for him.' I was convinced the woman was Sallie Stevens.

I backed up and parked a distance from the woman, wondering why I was doing this because I never stop for the boiled peanut couple or the smoked mullet man. I knew the woman. I was certain of that. I'd never seen her before, but she did remind me of Sallie. She seemed to glow, as if she were phosphorescent. I was haunted by her; somehow she was tied to me. I had a great need for contact with this sad-eyed woman under the green awning who seemed to be guarding her pile of darker green cabbages rather than trying to sell them.

'That's Sallie Stevens,' I said. 'I've got to talk to her.'

The woman's name was Gloria Gloria and she had been there for nearly ten hours, waiting. The man she had slept with for most of the winter and throughout the cabbage harvest had dumped the cabbages there at dawn and left in his truck. Abandoned her. Somehow I knew that others had done this before him. And even now, so soon after his leaving, the helpless, almost cowering, mask she wore when she was going with a man who pretended to be her savior, was gone, replaced by a time-worn hardness which cast itself over Gloria Gloria's young face. Now, as a direct result of ten hours' solitude, the skepticism returned to her green eyes, giving them a penetrating directness, which her next lover would recognize as a challenge, an inhibiting one, until she appeared to give herself over to him, the protector. It was only after she had been abandoned that Gloria's strength rose to support her, a glowing inner reserve which defined her and which she was unaware of, but which was her charm, her very spine. I was drawn to this woman. Gloria looked directly at me. I reacted to her, not with a challenge as a man might, nor with pity, but with genuine respect. But Gloria did not call the feeling respect, for she was so seldom treated in that manner. She had no word for my attitude toward her. What Gloria felt was equal to me as I was then, a tear-stained bedraggled mother of two young boys with my love-bug-spattered car and more stuff than she had ever owned in her entire life.

Though one could not describe this first encounter as anything other than a polite one, enough sympathy ran between us to unleash the boyishness in the boys. 'It's all right,' Gloria responded to Tom, who toed a cabbage; and she handed him a small crate to use as a goal.

Soon cabbages were scattered like giant green marbles over the white gravel.

I guessed she was in her mid-thirties. We said little as we stood together watching the boys kick cabbages. It was amazing to me. Here was a modern version of Sallie Stevens, the subject of my dissertation. She moved and talked and looked like my mental image of her, red black hair, dark eyes, an Irish plumpness to her round face and a devilish glimmer when she was secure or angry. Here she was with a pile of cabbages just as forlorn and abandoned as Sallie on her island, just as sad and hopeless, as dirty-pretty and time-worn as Sallie living on that island in the St Marys River waiting for her husband to return to her, a husband who couldn't have been much better than Gloria Gloria's man or my own husband.

His name was Nathan Atkinson, and he came to Georgia in the 1790s from the Carolinas where he had been tried and acquitted for murder. In Camden County he married Phereby Stevens. Less than a year later, he left her for Phereby's teenage daughter Sallie. They crossed the St Marys River together to get out of United States jurisdiction. I can only imagine what he did to make Sallie leave her home and mother, what he promised her, and how daring and adventurous she must have felt leaving home for Spanish territory to live on an island in Florida with a cattle thief and suspected murderer. It had to be physical. It was for me with Arthur. I imagine Sallie Stevens full of passion and romance. I also imagine her devastated at his leaving her alone on the island for months.

I have spent so much time thinking about that young woman that I am quite able now to visualize Sallie Stevens as a person, one who speaks and moves and makes love and cares for her children. This young woman I have read about is alive to me, and Gloria Gloria reminded me of her to such an intense degree that for a moment I thought Gloria was a reincarnation of her. But my Sallie Stevens is much more forlorn and much more dependent on love than Gloria is. They are alike, but different. There is a similarity. That's all. The young woman who came into my life from the early records is more like I am and would have admired Gloria Gloria as much as I myself admire her.

Sometimes I imagine that Sallie can move ahead in time from the island, Cabbage Swamp, where she lived in the 1790s and join me here; sometimes I imagine that Gloria and Sallie and I are all together, like sisters.

The boys were having a wonderful time kicking cabbages over the gravel. Both are towheads, unlike me with plain brown hair, unlike Arthur who is dark and almost viciously skinny. The boys are identical in size, though Tom is three years older and wears glasses. At his age he loses or breaks or outgrows about six pairs of frames and four sets of lenses a year. He wears a spectacle case on his belt which he forgets to use. Alan, the younger, lets himself be guided by his older brother; and so, as usually happens, the guide — even such a myopic one as Tom — breeds trust in the traveler, allowing him to explore a new, sometimes imaginary world without fear. Alan follows his near–blind keeper as a dreamer moves in a dream. And Alan takes after me.

A small cabbage rolled between Tom's legs into the crate. 'Goal!' Alan and I yelled in unison. 'Two points!'

As we talked, Gloria remained seated on her wooden crate surrounded by her cabbages. Simply cabbages. No cucumbers, no carrots, no avocados, no tomatoes. Cabbages only. I asked her how much she was selling them for, and she pointed at some pencil markings on her crate: 'Cabbages 10c.'

'They're fresh–picked,' she said. 'Yesterday. Yesterday morning.' She wore a thin white cotton dress, a farm girl's dress, stained and sweat streaked. The flimsy cloth stuck to her legs. Dampness ran like a trickle, beginning at a place between her breasts and spreading down across her stomach, making her skin show through. Dirt smeared her front, a swipe of black grease, axle grease, probably left there by a large hand swiping at her breasts.

I handed her a dollar bill.

'I don't have the change.' Her eyes were unable to disguise her lie, but she added, 'Take all you want. I'll never sell them before they rot.'

The cabbages were not in proper crates and appeared to have simply been dumped there on the white gravel. She gazed at the empty road while I walked around the pile hefting a dozen or so, pretending I knew something about cabbages. They looked identical to me.

Somehow I knew that this woman had no intention of waiting where she was (not as I, or Sallie Stevens, would have) near long enough to sell all those cabbages, nor did she plan to take them with her when she went.

'Where did you get so many?' I asked, holding up two. 'I don't believe I've ever seen so many all at one time. There must be thousands.'

'A ton and a half,' she said. 'He won't be back for them. And he won't be back for me, the bastard.' She had a soft voice. 'I didn't do anything to him. He just took off on me.'

Just took off. That is precisely what I had done with the children not an hour earlier. Took off. Being in motion, getting away, I realized then, did not rid me of the truth: I was the one who had left. Even though I was on the move with the boys, my predicament was the same as Gloria's. Our men were gone. Each of us was on her own.

I carried my cabbages to the car. Gloria followed, united with me in some strange, but not unpleasant, way. 'You have nice-looking children,' she said, stopping when I stopped, putting on that skeptical look again.

'Will you be all right here?' I asked her. My arms were

beginning to feel the weight of the cabbages. The boys had run ahead and were both in the front seat. Tom was playing with the turn signals. 'Will someone come along for you?'

She did not reply.

I was about to tell her that I was sorry but the car was too full, that we had had to leave Dixie, the boys' golden retriever, behind because there wasn't enough room for all of us with our belongings.

'What you got in the car?' she asked.

I froze for an instant, almost expecting this stranger to pull out some kind of cabbage knife, and forced myself to glare at her, looking directly into those dark huckleberry eyes. 'What do you mean by that?'

'Nothing. I always wonder what nice folks take with them when they run.'

'I left him,' I said, more sharply than I intended.

'I figured that. I've known a lot of runaway women and you don't look no different to me.'

'He made me,' I said, suddenly defensive for some reason.

Besides, I thought, I have a good reason and I have some place to go. He doesn't. That's why I am the one who left in the first place. Someone has to do the leaving.

But I knew I was running. The truth had begun to seep in. I always run. And I was doing it then. Maybe I always would. At the time, I was not ready to acknowledge that as the truth. Not ready to give in, not yet. I told myself that maybe once I got home I would take off the mask, stop running away and face myself.

'You're running all right,' Gloria said. 'Do you know how I can tell real quick? I look at the car. How it's loaded. You aren't going on any pleasure trip, that's certain. I can see you clear as a bell, breaking your rope and grabbing up those kids, getting your stuff together and getting your ass out of wher-ever you were. You got out of there in such a hurry you don't even know what you got in that car of yours, and I'll bet you

weren't half sure if you even had those kids with you for the
first ten miles.'

She was right about that. 'The first fifteen is more like it,' I
said, laughing. 'How did you know that?'

'It's a gift,' she said. 'I can get inside people. You're
running, that's certain.'

I admitted to her that I might be. 'But I had to leave him,' I
said, weakening. 'I didn't know what he was going to do next.
He got violent and shot up our trailer.'

'You in a trailer?' Gloria said. 'Where are you running to?'

'Saint Augustine.'

'What's there?' she asked me, as if she already knew the
answer.

'My grandfather,' said Tom brightly. 'He has a boat.'

'Home,' Gloria said. 'What are you going to do there?'

'I need to go back,' I told her. Then, I just blurted it out to
her, this stranger. 'I left my family too soon . . . before I was
ready.'

'My mother's a writer,' Alan said. 'She can make people
up.'

I still don't understand it. I was on trial before this woman,
this ageless woman in her rag dress which glowed even though
it had dirt streaked across its front. There was not the flush of
youth in her cheeks one expects in a young woman. Her body
was not firm nor skinny; it just looked used. There was a faded
scar on her cheek as if a cat had scratched her deep enough to
tear flesh, her flesh which was translucent, almost phosphorescent.

The little crop duster passed above us again, flying low,
heading back to the hangar. Gloria looked up at the sky,
saying, 'Now, that's the kind of job I'd want. You come in
twice, three times a year, spray for bugs, fertilize and you're
out of there with a wad in your pocket.' The small airplane
was obscured now by the thick growth of palmettos and kudzu
vine. The swamp forest softened the engine noise. 'Besides, a

person's happiest if she's flying, one way or another. No more
dirt farming for me.'

I backed away from her and touched the car.

'What's your name?'

'Gloria Gloria,' she said. 'Just call me Gloria.'

I couldn't resist her. 'Since you can't fly, then we would be
glad to give you a ride as far as Saint Augustine.'

'I stink pretty bad.'

I waved off the remark and Gloria went to recover her
belongings, a pair of shoes and a canvas bag. She fondled a
blue blanket for a moment before throwing it onto the pile of
cabbages. I couldn't hear what she said to the blanket.

'Get in the back, you two, and fasten your seatbelts.'

'That's Tom and that's Alan,' I said, once Gloria was in the
car.

'Nice,' Gloria said, turning and nodding at the boys who sat
stiff in the back seat each with a cabbage on his lap. 'Yes, they
are nice boys.'

'Is she coming with us?' asked Tom.

'Something smells,' Alan said.

'I do,' said Gloria. 'I can't help it.'

'Oh, that's okay,' said Tom, giving Alan the elbow.

To me, Gloria said, 'If you'll stop at a station, I'll clean
myself up. I haven't been around hot water in a while.'

As we drove away, leaving the green pile and the faded
green awning behind, Gloria wrapped her arms around
herself and, as if the car's motion had set her off, she began to
talk. 'He wasn't my husband or anything,' she said, motioning
with her thumb at the now vanished pile of cabbages. 'I've
been through that. He acted like he was, and for a while, at
first, I loved him so much it disgusted me. And he treated me,
at first, real nice, always saying how beautiful I looked. I
could be all puffed up from wine and sleeping on the ground
and awful smelling, worse than now, and he liked me that
way, at first anyway, wanting me and all, not complaining any

about the smells or the dirt, not even after a week or two weeks on the road.

'We were taking that load up to Atlanta in his truck. Then he got all tied up inside and dumped me on the road. I sat there all day and made three dollars and almost got raped once. And he's on his way to New Orleans with an empty truck. He'll get over there, sell the truck and spend the money on women not half as good as me. When he's broke, the potatoes will be ready and he'll have some other woman, run somebody else's harvester, get paid in cash and potatoes, buy another truck and dump the new woman and the potatoes on the road somewhere. I wish that son of a bitch hadn't left me there like heap of trash. He did it to me once before, the bastard, with watermelons. Watermelons sell. But he came back for me after he spent a couple of days in Lake City with the whores. Cabbages just sit there and stink. Pretty soon you start to stink right along with them while he goes off to New Orleans. I've spent so much goddamn time babysitting cabbages I look like a goddamn cabbage. Look at me. Just look at me. What do you see sitting over here? What am I? A stinking cabbage right from the bottom of the pile. That son of a bitch. I'm not going to live with a man like that ever again, not ever. I should have known when he did it to me with the watermelons, not to trust him with cabbages.' She closed her eyes. 'God damn, I stink.'

'We'll find you a place to wash,' I said. 'You can wear some of my clothes. I have plenty.'

'The next man I find, he won't own a truck,' said Gloria before she fell asleep.

As I drove home that afternoon with Gloria Gloria sleeping next to me, I tried to deny what I was doing. I pretended that what had happened an hour before was nothing more than another insignificant incident, one which I could chalk up as usual to Arthur's drinking, or his temper, or his insensitivity;

something I would not think important when I had settled down, or that gave me no real cause to pack up the children in the middle of the day firmly intending to leave him for good this time.

But, when I glanced over at the rag-tag woman, my own reasons — which I had tried to deny only moments before — took on tremendous force and did not seem groundless by any means. Something equally unforgivable had happened to her, and she was rid of her man. I realized for the first time that I was not being forced to stay with Arthur: I could leave him if I had to, and I did have to. What was I thinking? I had waited for months for the opportunity. Now I had it. There was something about her that gave me courage. Maybe it was right to do what I was doing, regardless of the guilt.

I asked myself what Sallie Stevens, the girl who was left alone for months on the island, would do now. Once she had found a canoe or a raft would she have gone straight to her mother's in Georgia? Yes. She would have run, as I was running then. Gloria was a lesson for both of us. Gloria was not running; she was moving on. But Sallie Stevens was not strong enough to leave the island and go anywhere else but home, and neither was I. I never learned whether Gloria still had a home she could return to — I never saw her again after that afternoon — but she would not have run there. She had developed some source of inner strength or spirit which no longer made it necessary for her to consider running. She may have been dirty and smelly just then, but she was strong — stronger than both Sallie Stevens and me put together.

And she could be made into such a pretty woman once again. Hair cut and permed; new clothes — blacks and reds were her colors. The life this woman led left her skin pale. Her face had the indelible marks of alcohol and weather and men. The bruise on her arm, a fresh one just above her left elbow, was the size of an over-large thumb print. I could easily visualize the man who had given that mark to her. He was not her master, he was simply stronger, physically, than she was.

He had a beer gut and tattoos on his shoulder blades and arms. He was selfish and quick in bed and cruel to her in public: weakness mocking strength. With just a few dollars she could turn herself into a knockout. Probably she was one when she was my age. Get her to wash her hair and cut it short, put her into a pair of my tight jeans and one of my red tank tops: that would take years off her — ten maybe. There was nothing wrong with her inside that I could tell; she just needed some primping outside. At least I was capable of doing something about that for her. I imagined what she would look like in my clothes.

She awoke and caught me looking over at her.

The vivid image I had of her looking like an older version of me, the picture I had in mind of her man, fled.

I watched the road, waiting for her to drop back to sleep. When she didn't, I asked, 'Do you have children, too?'

'One,' she answered crisply. 'I'm not sure where he is. Colorado, last I heard.'

There was another tractor ahead of us, but I had no need to pass.

'I had him when I was eighteen,' she said. 'In case you're interested.'

'That's how old I was when I had Tom. I got pregnant my spring semester in high school, but they let me graduate anyway. I was class valedictorian at the same time.'

'You look like you were,' she said.

'He looks a lot like you, I bet. Your child,' I said. For some reason I knew that already.

'Yes. Not quite so skinny. No taller. Same hair as me. It looks better on him.' She laughed for the first time.

I knew that, too. Same round face and translucent skin.

We passed through Penny Farms. Outside of Green Cove Springs, we stopped at the KOA Campground, and Gloria used her cabbage money for a shower. She accepted a pair of my jeans and a red tank top. While she cleaned herself up, the boys and I waited for her on the small boat dock, with sodas and candy bars.

There was no more complaining from the back seat.

'That helped,' Gloria said. 'Thank you for the clothes.'

And one after the other, the children nodded off. Soon, Gloria was asleep again. Her presence calmed me, gave me confidence in the correctness of my actions.

What else could Arthur have done? I thought. It was the possum's own fault. That animal shouldn't have crawled under our trailer in the first place. Besides, who could tell it was a 'she' and that she was pregnant? No one could. Not until after it was over. Maybe she was rabid, too. If not rabid, she was crazed — from confinement. After all, Arthur did try to coax her out from under.

Gloria's head lay on the window ledge and the wind was drying her hair.

Of course I knew. I knew perfectly well the possum was female and pregnant. She was looking for a place to have her babies. I knew that, and I told Arthur that, but he didn't want it under the trailer. We did try, or pretended to, calling and cooing. He put out bait — fresh eggs and tuna fish — and he sucked kisses that made my spine tingle, disgusting sucking kisses I'd never heard from him before. I was the one who suggested that he shoot it, if it bothered him so much. We argued.

Then I saw what was coming and held tight to the boys. I knew he had gone for his shotgun and stayed where I was watching the slow-moving possum, who by now was too crazed to play dead, crawl behind the butane tank at the front of our trailer by the hitch. I knew then that I should stop him and call the animal rescue league or the fire department who would use a live trap.

There was no need for Arthur to use the shotgun. There were plenty of other ways. But I froze, without protest, because I knew what he was going to do and I wanted him to do it. I wanted him to blast our stupid house trailer with both barrels, wanted him to pock the siding and tear it away from the rivets. 'Don't do it, Arthur,' I said.

Then I grabbed his arm and screamed. That made him lift the gun, just as he pulled the trigger, and blow out the living room window. I knew what I was doing. I screamed so he would go on shooting. I wanted to egg him on. I wanted it. 'Stop it!' I covered my ears. 'Stop it!'

The shotgun went off six, eight, ten times as he moved around to the far side of the trailer. Both tires went flat. By the time he ran out of shells, the animal was a wet scattering of bone and blood. The trailer's insulation puffed out below the bedroom window. The back of the couch in the living room was shredded.

Then he dropped the gun in the dirt and walked away.

I stopped screaming and watched him for a moment, not wanting to call to him. But I did.

'Come back here, Arthur! You rotten, rotten. . .'

Our neighbors in the trailer court kept their distance and watched him walking along the sandy road into the pine woods.

Then he did an odd thing. He turned with his hands cupped together and smiled. He opened his hands as if he were releasing a bird or something, raising his arms as if to follow the bird's flight. He leaned back and pointed. Then he shrugged and turned back toward the woods.

'You bastard!' I yelled. 'You rotten bastard!'

That was for the benefit of the neighbors.

Here was my chance. He had given me the excuse. We both were aware of that. In his mind, he had released his little bird from her bell jar. So I took him up on it. It wasn't bad enough when, a few months before, he set the bushes by the mailbox on fire, trying to burn out a wasp's nest with raw gasoline. That time he almost burned us up. But I didn't leave him that time, because the fire might have been a mistake. Instead I helped scrape the paint blisters and retouch the siding. Blasting our trailer and that little dance in the road with the invisible bird was no mistake. Now I was ready.

I quickly put the children in the car, making three or four trips, throwing the stuff in the back, hoisting suitcases and boxes onto the roof rack, tying down the load with the clothesline. By now, the fury had passed. I was calmer, more efficient. My mind raced with my body.

'Where's Daddy?' Alan asked, as I slowly drove toward the entrance gate, passing the neighbors who had retreated inside — all but Mrs McCloud, who stood by the road in her faded cotton dress signaling to me.

'Cookies for the boys,' she said, passing a bag through the window on Alan's side. 'Good luck to you, girl.'

'I have to leave,' I said to Norma McCloud.

'Of course you do,' she said.

'I just have to leave him,' I said. 'I can't stand it any more.'

'Of course you can't,' she said.

We left the trailer court for good.

'Where's Daddy?' Alan asked again.

'He went for a walk in the woods,' said Tom.

Four or five miles went by. The cookies vanished. Tom climbed into the front seat and Alan stretched out in back kicking my blow–dryer onto the floor.

'Where is Dad, Mom? Where are we going?' Tom touched my arm.

'I don't know,' and I didn't. For the first time.

I looked in the rearview mirror and saw Alan sleeping and was surprised that both of the boys were actually with me, that I hadn't forgotten one of them. Only then did I relax my grip on the wheel. 'He's working, probably,' I said. 'That's it. He probably went to work.' The tears began again. 'Sit quietly, darling. Let's let Alan nap. I don't want to talk about it just now. We'll be at Grandpa's soon.'

At first I drove fast as if he were chasing me. It wasn't until after we stopped alongside the pile of cabbages and took on our passenger that I kept to the speed limit.

Under normal circumstances, I would have driven straight through to St Augustine. I never pick up anyone on the road. There is something about hitchhikers that frightens me. Not the thumb, the eyes. As you get close, they either look right at you or they keep their eyes down so you can't see them. Women are the worst, the young ones. They look right at you. They cry to be picked up using only their eyes like they are lost and have become innocent children again. Then you let them off and you know they were thinking all the while that you are the biggest sucker the world has ever seen.

Maybe this woman sitting next to me was no different. She looked like a hitcher. But I think she was more than that. For all I knew about Gloria Gloria she had made it all up, wasn't dumped on the road with a truckload of cabbages, but was standing there in the shade waiting for a sucker like me to come along. But I doubt that because in the next few weeks I became convinced Gloria had been placed there, that she was waiting for me to come along when I did, and that she was expecting me. I found Sallie Stevens in the same way. I was researching outposts that the Spanish maintained on the St Marys River when Sallie Stevens appeared in the records.

She just flashed out at me from the microfilm on the reader as if she had been set down on Cabbage Swamp for me alone to find, as if she had set off a parachute flare just when I needed her most.

The same goes for Gloria. I am certain she was waiting for me that afternoon.

I believe that she was placed there to help me just when I needed her; placed there to remind me that life does unfold, that there is a plan. I had forgotten that, or rather, I knew it in my heart all along and in my spirit, but had forgotten. Life does unfold. It does. And nothing can stop it, because if you try and stop it, your spirit dries up and you become frightened and lost and you are left with confusion and solitude, slogging through a swamp.

We came into St Augustine on King Street. I woke Gloria up. Her hair was dry now and frizzed naturally. She looked good in my jeans and tank top, years younger in fact, almost like a student, a graduate student. I stopped at the plaza and opened my purse. 'You'll need some money.'

'You've done enough for me,' she said, but took the twenty, folding it and stuffing it into the pocket of the jeans.

'Where's the cabbage lady going?' Alan asked from the back seat.

Gloria stepped back from the car and waited for us to drive away. The Tradewinds was a few yards from her — across Cathedral and down Charlotte — and I knew that she would go there and find a man. She didn't have enough money for a motel room. 'She's not going anywhere,' I said to the children. 'She's staying here. And we are going to surprise Grandpa.'

'She looks like you, Mom,' Tom said.

'That's because she's wearing my clothes.'

'I don't mean that. She looks like you.'

I have no flesh and blood sisters.

'I like her,' Alan said. 'She talked to me.'

We all waved good-bye to Gloria Gloria, and I pulled into the traffic.

This is a tourist town. I always forget that until I get stuck behind one of the open sightseeing trains. We followed it past the International Doll Museum and north along the bayfront. It carried a dozen or so tourists. I feel superior and special, following the tourists and listening to the amplified patter of the drivers — re-discovering my home town by listening to the tourists listen and by watching the tourists watch St Augustine as it passes before them:

. . . and, on your right, is the Castillo de San Marcos. This is Saint Augustine's most impressive historical landmark and tells us a lot about the past. From the time of its founding, Saint Augustine always had a fort of wood, soon decayed and periodically rebuilt. Finally, as advancing English colonies to the north threatened to engulf Florida and Saint Augustine, officials in Spain authorized the building of this great coquina stone fortress here . . .

The fort is remarkable. I caught myself looking over to where Gloria had been sitting, wanting her to understand the importance of the Castillo, and was surprised to find that Gloria was not there. It was odd; the car didn't feel empty of Gloria, even though she was no longer there.

. . . Its construction was begun in 1672, a century before the Revolutionary War, and it was completed in 1695. The stone used in this fort, and later in many of Saint Augustine's buildings, is called coquina, a shell rock formation quarried on Anastasia Island.

'Probably she doesn't give a damn anyway,' I said.

The earth work at the west of the fort was once planted with Spanish bayonet, a yucca plant with sharp, saber-like leaves. . .

The sightseeing train turned left at the City Gate and the driver's voice began to fade. However, the sense I had of Gloria's presence did not fade.

. . . During the yellow fever epidemic of 1821, this half-acre plot was set aside as a public cemetery for the many protestant pioneers to the new Florida Territory. Often such burials, made at public expense, went unmarked. . .

We continued north on San Marco, past Ripley's 'Believe It or Not' Museum, past the entrance to Juan Ponce de Leon's Fountain of Youth Park.

I took a right on Locust Street.

'We are almost at my father's house,' I said. I wanted Gloria here, to give her a guided tour of my neighborhood.

'Who are you talking to, Mom?' Tom asked.

'Well, here we are.'

My childhood home is a white Carpenter Gothic on Water Street which overlooks Hospital Creek, the Matanzas River and, further out, the inlet into the Atlantic. That day the pink azaleas along the drive were still in bloom. Someone had been caring for the roses, Mother's roses. All of them were budding, the Cherokee by the house, the Loyalists and the Spanish Royals. The yard would be lovely for Easter. My father's ketch, the *Miranda*, was tied up to the dock which runs from the yard out across the salt marsh into Hospital Creek.

I let the boys out of the car and, without calling out a greeting, went through the kitchen, up the back stairs to my old childhood room, which shows no signs either of my motherhood or my marriage.

No recent photographs, no trinkets, no objects which can remind me of almost nine years of my life with Arthur. I stopped living in that room after the summer of my senior year in high school, and it has stayed the way I left it. Here I began to write stories before I got bogged down in academics; and here I have begun to write stories again.

I opened the window and leaned out. For a moment, it seemed that those two boys down there in the yard could not possibly be my boys; and I did not recognize my own sharp voice, warning those children of the river's current and the quirk of the tire swing on its flexible oak branch. Those taunts and cries of delight did not come from my children. For just that moment, leaning out the window, I was an innocent high school senior again.

Then a man with blond-white hair came into view, destroying the fantasy. He was dressed in white and wore a wide-brimmed planter's hat. I watched him cut across the lawn to shake hands with Tom and Alan before kissing them. Then they moved toward the house, deep now in conversation.

'Hey! Hey, Daddy! Here I am. I'm up in my room,' I called like a little girl left out.

He looked up at me. The boys hung on his cuffs and sleeves. 'Well, if it isn't Rapunzel,' he called.

'I'll be right down!'

First he held me close. 'Nancy!' Then he held me at arms' length. 'You are a sight. What? Did you have your hair cut?'

'I'm sure the boys have told you everything by now,' I said, hugging him. 'The blabber mouths. I'm sorry I didn't call you first, but we left in sort of a hurry. Unexpectedly.'

We looked at each other seriously for a moment, knowing there were questions between us that had to be asked and answered.

'Where is Arthur?'

'He didn't come.'

'He shot our house with his shotgun,' Alan said.

My father pretended not to hear that. Instead, playing the indulgent grandfather, he let the boys go through his trousers for change before sending them back to play on the tire swing.

'I'm afraid you're on your own this evening,' he said. 'I have plans.'

'I can see that you do, Daddy. You're all spiffed up. Where did you get that hat?'

It amazes me how my father can turn suddenly boyish. He was blushing and his eyes avoided mine. The next thing he'd be scuffing the lawn with his shoe like an abashed high school kid.

'I won't be too late,' he said, almost apologetically.

'You look great, Daddy. I didn't mean . . . you must be happy. You look it.'

'How long are you staying with me this time?'

'I don't know. A while. You don't mind, do you?'

He threw open his arms to embrace the enormous house, the ketch, the dock and river, the yard, and even the sidewalk and street out front, the flowers and grass.

'Stay as long as you like,' he said. 'What do you think I keep this place up for? Not for myself.'

We both looked at the boys on the swing. Tom was pushing Alan who was inside the tire with his feet dangling above a worn spot on the grass.

'You won't have to babysit,' I said. 'Tom is very good with Alan. But sometimes I swear he acts like his father. I can leave them together though, and they're fine. We won't be a burden or anything. I don't want to finish school.'

Father didn't hear that. He checked his watch.

'Move your car, will you, honey? It's time for me to go.' He looked at me for a moment, wanting to ask something, but instead he said, 'I'm not sure what there is in the kitchen. You'll have to pull some kind of supper together yourself. I don't eat at home much these days.'

'I don't want to finish school,' I said again, urgently. 'I don't care about getting my degree. I don't need it any more. I wasn't getting it because I wanted it. Arthur thought I should get it to keep me busy. It wasn't my idea in the first place.'

But he was already in motion toward his car. 'We'll talk about it when I get home, if it's not too late. It's sad Arthur can't be here with you.'

He knew that Arthur was with another woman.

I have come home alone before.

This time I am home for good.

I must be home for good.

He knew about her. It wasn't the Cajun woman that hurt. What hurt was that there had been so many. And now there was another one. After the Cajun woman was finished with, he would want me for a while, and then there would be yet another one. He would go on. Then I would let him come back, as I always did, because it was so wonderful when he did: I knew I would let him come back. That's what hurt, and my father knew how many times I had been hurt by him and how many times I had let him come back. But this time, it was different: my anger was gone. I must have looked a sight that afternoon. No wonder Father wanted to get away from me.

'You still love him, don't you?' he asked. 'You're not splitting up or anything like that?'

'I don't know,' I said.

Still, no matter what I said — love him or not — I was afraid that I would let Arthur come back to me. And that is what I could not do. No matter what, I had to gain the strength to turn him away when he came for me.

Then, only to stop my father from worrying, I said, 'I want to love him, Daddy.'

'Well, that's good.'

Automatically without thinking I untied the boxes and luggage from the roof and separated my stuff from Tom's and Alan's and carried the boys' bags and boxes into the house.

As usual, the boys would make their mess in the guest room at the back of the house over the living room and would sleep on the screen porch which overlooked the river.

There had always been twin beds on the sleeping porch. The huge live oak tree in the yard shelters the place, isolating it, taking it into its limbs and holding it like a nest high above the ground in a dark green forest. I slept there often as a young woman, pretending I was alone in a forest waiting for a man to come to the nest I had made there for us. I knew what I would say to the man and do with him long before there was a real one there on the sleeping porch in the trees with me, and I imagined how it would make me feel. Lying there alone and naked under the leafy green canopy, I wished for the adventure of a real man in my nest, and one day I got my wish.

It came in the form of a large-shouldered man who was waist deep in the surf, casting a mullet net by the City Pier. I had ridden my bicycle over the bridge to the island to watch the sunrise. I watched him cast. His shoulders fascinated me. I left my bicycle and climbed down the rocks onto the sand to be closer to him. Then, on one cast he captured a full net of silvery mullet. Even he was not strong enough to drag the net ashore. There must have been thirty or forty fish from that single cast. He looked around for help and that's when he noticed me.

I waded into the surf not knowing what he wanted me to do, unaware of the water and the foam. I was standing next to him, chest deep in water. The net writhed with so many fish.

He was calm. His dark beard was silvery with water and sun. He told me to grip the top while he tied the net closed, and together we pulled the fish toward shore.

We put the fish in coolers. When that was finished, I suddenly felt wild. I didn't want to leave because I would never see him again. I searched for an excuse to hold on to him. What I came up with was feeble, but it got me what I wanted. I told him that I was too wet to ride my bicycle home; I didn't want to get chafed. I knew no one was home — Father always golfs with my uncle Jack on Saturday mornings — and I planned to give him breakfast if he wanted it or just coffee if he wasn't hungry. But both of us were hungry and we used the sleeping porch, my nest. And it was there when I told him about my mother and about White Dove, my cat, who had died, too, but whose life was a string of accidents, just like our meeting was an accident and our being there on the sleeping porch was an accident. I held him and told him about how White Dove was first run over by a car that broke her pelvis and both front legs, how she was shocked when she was chewing an extension cord, how she had caught her tail on fire three times in the kerosene heater. I told this man, this fisherman called Arthur Meade, all the details. About how there were no scars on White Dove. About how she had lost some of her fur in places and liked baths and a blow–dryer. And I remember so well the exciting feeling when Arthur began to blow on my skin, softly blow, until I wanted him again. After that when he wanted me he called me 'Cat'.

I had such a vivid memory of us there on the sleeping porch that Saturday morning when Father was playing golf that I put down the boys' suitcases and sat on the bed.

'I will take care of you,' Arthur promised me. 'I will protect you and take care of you.'

He had made a promise.

Now I don't need his protection nor his doctor-like caring. I wanted his love, that's all, but he could not give me that. Now I am gradually learning not to want him at all, not to melt when he says to me over the telephone, 'Come on. Come on, Cat. For old time's sake.' Don't. Don't, I say to myself. You are not his cat. You do not want him. No. Don't do it. Don't go back to him again.

Please, Arthur, please don't call.

chapter 3

March 16

The journal is not the fashionable medium these days in which to display one's soul. The psychiatrist's couch or therapy or the peer-support group is the recognized forum. We are considered anti-social if we prefer to keep our soiled laundry out of the public washer. So then, I am anti-social; I will not heave and wrench myself before others. I am not anxious to make my private self known at all, but I must. Simply put, I have always kept a journal because there is a healing which comes from clearly stating one's feelings, transforming vagueness into language, pain and joy into the written word. I suppose the same healing occurs other ways, but I prefer this method and write here now with the single purpose of healing my wounded soul, so that I may (as Yeats says) 'myself remake'.

Two things:

First, my wife is not what you call a 'nice-nice' person. She can fool you. She looks like one: dark hair, good clothes, smooth skin, trim figure (even after two kids), good bones, photogenic, okay at sports (golf and tennis, a little sailing), but underneath she is not one of your upper-middle class cynics. She may be lucky, rich and well cared-for like one; but she is not nice-nice.

Second, when her mother died she needed someone. Her father was a basket case for years, so I became her father substitute. We do tend to fall in love with the women we have rescued. She began as my chipped porcelain high school girl and neither of us could kick the role. She became the little silly college girl, the little fawning graduate student, the good and helpless mother so precious. While I was the Magic Professor. The Professor of Comparative Literature. Here comes Doctor Meade to save the day.

We did that for almost nine years because we didn't know how to get out of it, and there didn't seem any reason to try. It was safe: I was the savior, she was the nice-nice mother. I ignored the fact that Nancy was also a deeply religious woman of the variety William James might describe as being weighted in temperament on the side of the darker aspects of the universe and fatally forbidden to linger, as those of the opposing temperament do linger, over cheer and pathological optimism. Her name does not suit her temperament at all: she is more of a Renée.

While Nancy might attempt a delightful vision or a cheerful thought, her temperament, her nature, is bleak. I suppose that is what interested me about her to begin with. I love my wife, and I attempt here a song of that love. Although I treated her as a wounded bird — too fragile, too delicate, too beautiful — she was never my bird.

My love for her is humiliating. I understand her. She is not stable, she is easily unstrung, she has delusions; but they are a part of her heritage. All the women in her family were raised, fed and clothed on delusions. Her future well-being from this day forward depends upon her ability to perpetuate those delusions. I don't envy her. 'It's so, if you think it's so,' has become her way of life as it was her mother's and her grandmother's. She has chosen to separate herself from the rational. She has chosen the superstitious and the mystic which are so suited to her dark soul. Our lives are difficult; I suppose each of us makes his decision toward entropy, toward the path of the easiest spiritual rest. We do not resist that which puts our souls at ease.

My disease is not the mystic, but the self-conscious. She accuses me of being crisp, dry, removed, an idea to myself. With them gone — my family, my flesh — I am little more than an idea. Nancy might say: 'I am lost without my family. He is not my family. So nothing is lost as I go to seek my light.' As I said before, she is a bleak soul, a dark soul, a sad soul. As for me, the flesh in my life has departed. Wife gone. Sons gone. I am lost without them. They will not return. Thus I must fabricate for myself a new frame in which to live.

She has gone to seek her spiritual ease in the heritage of her family.

I am the one who was left behind. I must not become bitter.

Her path is most difficult. The trappings she carries with her, the American girl trappings of her money and good looks, her health and her spit-and-shine-smile mask a dark soul.

Who cares about a glum rich girl? She has gold and beauty and youth. Who takes her tears seriously, this sad rich American girl with a pain like a gaudy orchid displayed for us to see?

I have sympathy for her. She is my wife, still. More important, I love her. Yes. I love her. Certainly I realize better than anyone that she is not a pathological optimist. But she is passionate, honestly passionate. Her pain is real. And I have lost her, not to another man, but to her family and her family's superstitious ways . . .

I have moved. On my porch swing with a bottle of whiskey I now let the fire ants crawl on my shoes and bite my ankles just to see how long I can take it, to see how much of the redneck in me has remained. The pain is hot, the poison makes my ankles ache, but I am alive. My heart works. With her and the boys gone, I just might go back to my own people and find a woman I understand easily — a dark redhead with dark skin and dark eyes, an Irish-looking woman who has the Cajun dancer way about her. She will be glad to sit here, sweaty and drinking from the same bottle. She knows for sure what's good for both of us without having to stop and think about it first.

PART 2

chapter 4

With Mother gone, I used the back stairs all through high school, and ducked into my little room, not venturing into any of the other rooms upstairs, for my father had put them all to sleep. When I came to visit him — as I often did without Arthur, especially for the past five or six years — my father put the boys in the guest room, the only room upstairs besides mine which someone, I have never known who, kept dusted and relatively free of must and mildew. My father always said that he didn't mind it if the boys were up there. 'Memories do not touch small children,' he said, but he didn't go up there himself. He would call good night to us from the bottom of the steps, and I can still hear his voice, deep and rich, filling the staircase from the hall off the living room.

Now he was using the master bedroom again; the upstairs was open and aired. I would not have been surprised if he had padded down the hall when he had returned from his date on my first night home and looked in on the boys, Alan flat on his back fully clothed and Tom curled up on his pillows.

The corridor leading to my room was no longer dark. There was life in the house once again, after years and years. I was certain that there must be more than one person living here, for one person alone could never make the house, vast as it is, feel so entirely occupied. My father's house was no longer a dark shell where he lived in the den like a caretaker; he was now using all of the fifteen rooms, or at least I thought I could detect use and presence in each of them. I explored the living room, the small bedroom off the den, the sitting room and the library. Although the long walnut table in the dining room was covered and was not ready to be set for dinner, there were two chairs pulled up to it, and place mats and silverware were on the sideboard. He did say that he didn't eat at home much these days. In the library, newspapers, junk mail and magazines covered most of the surfaces; the oval and square framed photographs of Mother were gone; the curtains were open. A woman's touch.

How young my father seemed with his blush and scuffing toe in the grass, trying to make me believe that he was not anxious in the least to go wherever it was that he was dressed to go with his planter's hat, wanting me to believe that he would much rather stay with us. If his eyes had ever danced with youth before, I had been too young to see how anticipation revealed itself on Father's face and in his eyes. 'So,' I said to no one in particular. 'He really is with someone. Good for him.'

I stood in the hall for a moment listening for the boys. The only sound came from the television.

This big white house — the place where I live even when I am living elsewhere — is set back from the street in the magnolias and live oaks, resting on its enormous lawn. I do not wish to own this house, although it will pass on to me upon my father's death. I have no need to covet this house. I am in no hurry, for the house is mine — an extension of myself. This house has nothing to do with Arthur. I am supposed to live here. In my heart, I have always lived here. Anywhere else I have been a visitor, a camper, a squatter. I am not like Arthur, not the kind to live and die in a trailer. I will not return to him there, not even if he has replaced the windows and patched the holes. I hope I have become strong enough to stay away from him. I belong here.

Here I feel no need to finish my dissertation — not because I am lazy or afraid, but because the academics no longer excite me. The passion I once felt for research has gone cold. Here I can be. Feel. Revive myself. Maybe I might accomplish something imaginative, creative here . . . piano lessons again. All Arthur was concerned about was how my assistantship would dry up if I abandoned my dissertation, and who would pay my share of the living expenses and the babysitter. He would only laugh at my thought of piano lessons. The warmth here, the security, makes me want to take a chance. Even if what I have decided to do takes a long time or if I fail, I will at least have tried something new, something I care about. Here, at least, I am allowed to search for what I care about. Here I can try.

In my room I lay on the bed and immediately missed him.

Maybe resentment quickly evaporates. Why do I feel this way? I made him do it so he could set me free. Did I? Is that why I am here? Maybe he did it. Maybe I forced him into a corner, making him get out that ridiculous shotgun, knowing full well he was going to blast himself out of our lives by giving me a valid excuse to come here where I belong.

I kicked off my shoes.

That son of a bitch. You don't do that to somebody you love.

Maybe he did it so I could leave. Maybe he knew that if he shot out the windows and blasted the siding and blew out the tires, I would leave him. Maybe he wanted me to leave him, so he could go that Cajun woman. Maybe he knew I wanted to leave him and he finally let me, opened the door for me.

Do you do that to someone you love?

Then the house enveloped me once again; I was not on the road guarding a pile of cabbages, but here. Safe.

Perhaps a man can live in a place like that, but not a woman with a husband and two children.

We both made it happen. It's nobody's fault.

God, I hated that trailer. I deserve better than that. I deserve this.

Then, Gloria Gloria appeared before me, surrounded by rotting cabbages. 'I don't deserve this,' I heard Gloria say.

Yes. I deserve it here. I don't deserve a man like him. I will not go back to him.

Gloria stayed in my room with me for a little while.

'I hope I am not disturbing you,' she said.

'No,' I said. 'You are not disturbing me. I'm glad to see you.'

This would happen often in the next few weeks.

I dreamed of Gloria, saw Gloria at odd times in quick flashes: even while I was talking to someone else, I spoke with Gloria. That night I had my first dream of her, this woman my children called the Cabbage Lady. Later, I began to write down my dreams and our conversations.

I folded my arms and crossed my feet and did all I could to keep her there with me, but after a moment the figure of the woman, which looked like a cloud reflected in the bureau's mirror, dissolved and was replaced by the sound of the television in the children's room.

For dinner I found some eggs and spinach and cheese. An omelet for me. Grilled cheese for the boys. Good. A bottle of chablis.

Even as I prepared dinner, I could feel Gloria drifting in and out of the kitchen. This did not alarm me. Normally, at a quiet time like that, Sallie Stevens — the woman who once lived on the island in the St Marys called Cabbage Swamp — would have visited me. We used to carry on a natural conversation together in the kitchen of the trailer. Commiserating mostly, I realize now. Sallie Stevens' husband was gone most of the time, leaving Sallie abandoned on the island; and Arthur was gone too. We both needed someone to talk to. Sallie and I talked most of all about how we coped, how we managed without our husbands and why we didn't just leave them flat. We complained and bitched about absent husbands and made sly reference to how good it felt when our men came back to us. And it was good when they came back. I waited many nights, hot and moist, knowing Arthur would soon come home for me. Sallie said she did too. She told me about Nathan Atkinson, her husband the cattle thief, and how he left in the canoe and how he came home weeks later to bed down with her. And Sallie made my life in that trailer bearable. So I was used to 'calling up' Sallie — that's what I name it — for a chat, heart to heart. I used to close my eyes and call her up, coaxing her to appear. So when I closed my eyes and called her up this time, I was not surprised — not really, and certainly not alarmed — when it was Gloria's red tank top, followed by her face, vivid now and surrounded by a glow of sparkling white, that appeared before me in the kitchen by the refrigerator.

I was eating and mistook what I recognized as Gloria's voice for a sudden increase in volume of the television.

'What kind of a woman are you? The marrying kind or the affair kind?' she asked me. 'You should at least know that much about yourself.'

It was good to have her there with me.

'I've never had affairs,' I said. 'Not any.'

'Give it a try. Pretend you are in an old movie serial. Nobody gets hurt in them.'

'You mean, have men one after the other?'

'Sure. When it's over, it's over,' Gloria said. 'Why make it different from the way it is?'

'I don't want it to be over.'

'See. That's your problem,' said Gloria. 'Why did you leave him then? Why did you run? There goes the phone. Don't worry. It isn't him.'

A few seconds later the telephone did ring. I didn't expect Arthur to call, not for two or three days at least. But he could be in trouble. I let it ring three times anyway.

'Excuse me a minute,' I said to her. 'I'm going to answer it.'

It was the security service calling for my father. The panel showed a burglar at the Fountain of Youth Park's building number two. They couldn't locate my uncle Jack. 'I don't know what to do about it,' I told the operator. 'Can't you call somebody else?'

'We show a break-in at the gift shop,' said the operator.

'Don't you have another number to call?'

'Miller,' she said. 'Lee Ann Miller.'

'Lee Ann Miller,' I repeated.

'She's on the list. So are you. Ben Phillips. So is Jack Phillips. I tried him first.'

'Call the woman then.'

I hung up. Arthur wouldn't call — not for a few days. He would be out with our friends trying to line up as much sympathy on his side as he could. Good luck, Arthur!

Fat chance he had of getting sympathy from any of my friends. For years the women I know have been amazed I could tolerate my brilliant unstable womanizing redneck professor husband Arthur Meade with his piercing blue eyes and his wandering hands and quick perceptions which he articulated so fast and so naturally. His brutal tongue, his fox-quick mind, his piercing exaggerations. Who would sympathize with a man who turned a shotgun on his own home? Who would care for a wandering hound dog with a hot nose and a messy past?

What a wonder the boys weren't harmed!

What a relief to be where I belong. To be safe.

Even before the shotgun, it was horrid.

'Right,' said Gloria. 'You had to leave him. Otherwise you would have gone numb for the rest of your life, froze up and stayed that way. Stuck.'

I thought briefly of Sallie Stevens on that island, of me stuck in the trailer. Sallie Stevens had stayed stuck, gone numb, fallen asleep there on Cabbage Swamp.

'We had a marriage by default,' I said in defense.

The kitchen was silent.

It remained silent. I poured a glass of wine before I spoke to Gloria again.

'We did have a marriage by default,' I said to her. 'You can make fun of it if you want to. I had no one to turn to after Mother died, and my father closed himself up tight. He shut up the house. All through high school I was lonely. The only person who had any interest in me was Arthur. He made me feel better; I made him feel better. And I needed someone. I always do. I gave in to him because I couldn't help it. What's wrong with that?'

I knew the answer: I let him flatter himself with my need. But I waited for Gloria to tell me.

'It happens all the time.'

'So?'

'Besides,' I said. 'He did help me. After Mother died, the family fell apart. I needed him.'

'He came along at a convenient time. I've had men like that,' Gloria said.

'I really loved him,' I said. 'I was crazy about him until a few years ago.'

I waited for Gloria's response, which did not come. So I said it for her. 'He helped when Father couldn't. I was a good wife. A good faculty wife too. Until I made him do what he did to get rid of him.'

Yes. That was the truth. The words sounded like a song. This is how I describe the end of my marriage, how I sing it, just like this: I was a good wife, or tried to be. I was a good faculty wife, as well, which wasn't that easy. I was a good wife, until . . . I was able not to need him any more. Until he did what he did. There were other women as well.

That's how I described the break-up to my father when he came home that first night. It was almost convincing. The marriage by default idea made me out to be weak — a victim — but it was best not to mention to Father how from that first summer after high school onward Arthur liked to make love with me on the screen porch, better not to mention the power his desire had over me and how it enhanced and increased my own desire when it came to actually making love.

Then came Gloria again: 'There are men who would ache to sleep with you. There are men who would never be satisfied to live in a trailer court, men whose pride would not let them start a life with you in one, let alone stop there. Why can't you see yourself as valuable?'

'Wait a minute. What are *you* going to do, Gloria? You're in a worse spot than I am. What are you going to do? What do you have? I have this house.'

Wondering about Gloria, where she was right then, what she was doing, was a help.

By this time, it was dark outside. A single shaded bulb burned over the table in the kitchen. I sat there brooding, listening, arguing with Gloria. I might have been playing poker at the round table or hearts with a ghost.

Other men, I thought, other men don't grab for their shotguns and blast away at their homes. Had I driven him to that extreme? He'll pay for it anyway. If he thinks he can get away with that one. It's half my trailer, too. And he's going to pay. He's going to pay to have it fixed and pay what it costs to sell it. And if he sells that trailer without fixing it up just like new, he's going to take the loss and give me back what I put into it. Three thousand. I'll get that much back.

'That's the spirit,' Gloria said. 'I have to go. I don't have a place to sleep tonight.'

Then the kitchen was silent except for the rheumatic noise of the old refrigerator's compressor. The noise reminded me of the refrigerator in the trailer. Fantasies of the abandoned trailer, of vines growing through the shattered windows, of vandals and animals came to me. I saw the yard, now overgrown, invading the interior, causing a jungle with rotting beds, a highchair covered with slime, snakes, water in the toilet bowl green and alive.

But Arthur won't let the place rot. He stands to lose as much as I do. The burden of recovery lies squarely upon him.

He can sell the place for four without getting it fixed up, and I will still get my three. Either way, he'll pay. He'll pay with sweat or cash to repair the place, or he'll lose two thousand. He'll pay, one way or another. . .

My father found me there at the kitchen table. He looked away from the bottle of wine and the filled ashtray.

'Where are the boys?'

'They went to sleep hours ago.'

Actually, I had no idea when the boys had switched off the television or how long ago it had been since the house turned quiet and peaceful, as it always does when children fall asleep. It was some time after Gloria had left. My eyes held his for a moment.

'Thanks, Daddy,' I said. 'Thanks for taking us in.'

I stood and kissed his cheek.

'Where's your date?' I asked him.

'Date?'

'Your lady friend. Whatever.' I tugged at my white shorts.

'She's down on the dock. When we saw the light on, I wanted to be certain you were . . .'

'Presentable.' I crossed my arms in front.

'. . . awake first and felt like company,' he said. 'We'll talk in the morning.'

'I feel like company. I've had all evening to mope. I don't want to feel sorry for myself. Now, I'm ready to get angry. I'm going to leave him, Daddy. I mean it this time. I've been a good wife. I was a good wife, or I tried to please him. I was a good faculty wife — a damn good one. I was a good mother, which isn't that easy. I was good in bed. I was even good after he did what he did. The other women didn't kill it for me, not at first. But he didn't stop. I hung on as long as I could, but he kept bringing in more women, one after another. And I let him. I buried my hurt, and I let him do it. I hate myself for that, for being so weak. I'm disgusted with myself. I had to leave him. I couldn't stand myself any more.' I reached for my wine. 'Sure I feel like company. Bring on your lady friend.'

'Better in the morning. She'll be sleeping here tonight.'
Father put on a blue nylon windbreaker and turned up the
collar. 'Her name is Lee Ann. Lee Ann Miller. You'll meet her
in the morning.'

I told him about the telephone call from the security
service. He had taken care of it.

My father is a large man and he seemed larger then in his
windbreaker. 'You could use some sleep, sweetheart.' His
voice is gentle. 'We'll talk about this in the morning.'

That night I sat at my desk and called up Gloria. I closed my
eyes and called her. I didn't talk with her; she wasn't like
Sallie Stevens who was lonely and wanted to talk. So I
watched her. I watched her sitting alone under the open-air
tile-roofed building in the plaza downtown. I listened to her
listen to the skateboarders wheeling around the gazebo. I felt
the chill that Gloria felt when the sun set behind Government
House and watched her become more and more solitary in her
red tank top, watched her become prey to the locals cruising
the plaza.

But, as I watched Gloria sit there alone, Sallie Stevens came
to me. I know what she would have done. She would have
waited for Nathan Atkinson. That was in the documents I had
researched for my dissertation. Also, I know what I would
have done. Waited for Arthur. That was in my journal which
I kept when I camped at Cabbage Swamp where Sallie
Stevens had been. The island is joined to the mainland now,
no longer isolated in the St Marys River as it was in 1795. I
camped and worked at the Cabbage Swamp Wild Life
Management Area during the muzzle–loading season last
year. I worked weekends from mid-November through January — it was a job to get away from Arthur. The job also
brought me closer to Sallie Stevens.

I was hired for the deer season. The area was open only on
weekends. The only weapons allowed were muzzleloaders

charged with black powder. I was on duty at the management area from two and a half hours before sunrise until an hour after sunset, checking hunters into and out of the area, weighing, measuring, tagging their kill.

One of the first mornings I was on duty, a hunter pulled up to the tin-roofed check station at about 4:15 a.m., before I was open. He was a well-dressed hunter for that hour in the morning and had the appropriate weapon — a muzzleloader. He was fully camouflaged from hat to boots — coat, shirt, scarf, t-shirt and (I suppose) underwear. Where his t-shirt left off, his neck and face were painted with the same pattern in green, gray-green, and brownish tan, not smudged and blurred under the eyes like runny mascara the way most hunters are. I took his license, exchanging it for a numbered badge, and let him into the area.

Later that day he came out with no kill. Then he hung around the check station until the last hunter had gone. I invited him into the small one-room cabin. He was a graduate student in archaeology conducting a survey of the river channels in the southeast and showed me step by step on a map he had with him how the southern bank of the St Marys had moved north thousands of yards in two hundred years, leaving the ground we stood on high and dry. On the map he outlined the management area, showing me that the place had once been an island in the middle of the St Marys River. On the map, almost on the exact spot where we stood, someone had written two names — 'Sallie Stevens' and 'Nathan Atkinson'. The map must have been used for the 1793 census taken by the Spanish.

Of course the names were familiar. The Spanish language documents I had been using showed that Sallie Stevens had lived on Cabbage Swamp from 1792 until 1795 or beyond (her name disappears from the records) with Nathan Atkinson, a known cattle thief and spy.

For four months from Thursday night through Sunday I left the boys with Arthur and lived alone in the solitude that Sallie

Stevens must have lived. I came to know the marshes and hammocks in the slash pines. I came to know Sallie Stevens of Cabbage Swamp.

I cannot describe the first deer of the season because there were so many. Besides, the hunter, himself a seasoned veteran, initiated me as if I were (which I was in that at least) a virgin. Though I politely wished all hunters good luck, I was not sincere because their killing a deer meant that I was brought out of my reveries and required to perform a series of data collection activities. I gave the dead animal a number and a kill date. I recorded the sex. If it was a male, I measured and described the rack and counted the points. I weighed the animal. Then I rolled it on its back and, with an instrument which looks like a 'V', removed half of the jaw, for determining age. From the intestines I took an abomasal sample and examined the lungs for worms and the kidneys for fat. Then I shoveled the guts into a pit. During slow times in the afternoon I cleaned the flesh away from the gum line before adding the numbered jawbone to the jawbone bucket inside the check station. By mid-way through the season, I could take care of a kill in just under twenty minutes, and I estimate that during my time on Cabbage Swamp I took care of more deer than Sallie Stevens did herself during the three years she was a virtual captive on the island.

I have asked myself a number of times why I was not disgusted by all the death and blood, by the proud and blood-lusting hunters. My heart never failed to sink when I saw yet another hunter dragging his kill out of the woods, yet I didn't understand why I actually felt better rummaging through the lukewarm cavity of a five-point buck feeling for the heart and kidneys, than I did sitting in front of the check station alone gazing at the bright blue sky above the slash pine and oaks.

One afternoon, during a special two–day doe season, I was gutting a small pregnant doe which had been shot once in the throat so that she had bled herself to death on the run. The area below the diaphragm which separates the lungs and heart from the kidneys, stomach, intestines, reproductive tract and so forth was not touched by the lead ball, so there was virtually no blood in her upper chest or in the abdominal cavity when I went in for the samples. I cut away her teats; slit open her belly and was able to see all of her inner workings — I was suddenly amazed, literally wonderstruck, by how beautiful she was inside, all pinks and creams and whites and blues and purples.

It seemed that time was suspended and all thoughts of the circumstances of her slaughter as well as the excitement of the hunter, who was still pale from the thrill, left me while I concentrated — it was a meditative concentration — upon the large and small intestine, the white fat that surrounded the kidneys (unusual for a pregnant doe).

We are much the same inside: there is only a thin covering which separates our hearts from the hands of others. Our own hearts may be lifted from our bodies and examined or torn as easily.

I remember saying to the hunter, 'Look! See how beautiful she is!' And I also remember the hunter, his face still pale, turning away to be sick.

Then time began to move again.

I have carried that spectacle with me ever since; to understand that we are all vulnerable somehow gives me strength. I feel blessed in some way to have held the heart of that deer in my hands.

When I was not collecting biological data at the check station, I worked on my study of Sallie Stevens. What I know of her and of Nathan Atkinson comes from the documents which I have pieced together.

In July, 1792, Nathan Atkinson took Sallie Stevens and her two young brothers across the St Marys from Temple, Georgia, to a place called Cabbage Swamp in Spanish territory where he went to live with this teenage girl in what the records call 'fornication'.

The Sallie I imagine is eighteen — my age when I married Arthur.

She is frozen in my mind. She is alone most of the time. She cares for two young children. She gazes now and again onto the waters of the St Marys looking for her Nathan. His returnings fill the young girl with dread. He will return only to abandon her again.

It took me some time to understand what makes me ache so for my Sallie.

I see her on the riverbank watching him row toward her.

I am with her. We both know his coming means his leaving.

His shoulder muscles glisten with sweat. We ache for him. He glances over the bow to check his course and sees his woman standing there ankle deep in the St Marys. She does not call to the youngsters because she wants him for herself first.

He has not faded from her thoughts, and his presence becomes now heightened and more vivid. She can never let him fade. If she allows him to fade, upon his return she would be looking at a stranger. They would not know each other, and she would be lost. She would be slave to a stranger.

The vision I have is not a still-life one: Sallie stands motionless on the riverbank watching; it is Nathan Atkinson who moves — the sun sparkles on the oars. His shoulders are massive. He smiles and rows faster. She waits for him only to make love with him again. She has no place to go.

Just as I hold sacred the spectacle of life which was revealed by the heart of the doe, and just as I ache for Sallie Stevens watching her Nathan's shoulders, I once held an aching rage, a violent lust, for my husband. When I was in such a state, I tried harder to please him and, in doing so, I pleased myself more — was not cold inside as I am now toward him — was able to lose myself with him.

Our physical attraction was once enormous. When I was at Cabbage Swamp alone, he would surprise me and take me inside the check station on the floor. I began to wait for him to come to me — as Sallie must have waited, not knowing if he would come — waited for our cries and sweat and that passionate darkness which is so wonderful and frightening, always like a new adventure.

At times, I actually believed that I was Sallie Stevens and he was my Nathan.

I stood outside the station as she must have stood on the riverbank. When I saw him at a distance driving along the causeway, I went inside to undress and wait for him.

When he would leave, I watched his car as if it were Nathan's canoe moving — the paddle rising and falling as he stroked. I stood motionless for what seemed like hours until he disappeared down the long straight causeway.

I did not move until he was gone. Each time I waited until he was out of sight.

But once I did move.

He finished with me quickly. He dressed. I had the impression that he had someplace else to go. I knew where he was going but did not want to know it.

That time I did not wait. I went about my routine even before he had the car turned around. I let myself forget about him immediately. I did forget about him, and he became a stranger. He was not on my mind. I didn't miss him. I was free of him for a while. Free of him.

The excitement I felt was frightening. It did not matter to me if he returned or not. I was able to carry on without him. For the first time, I was able to live without holding him in my mind — holding him because I was afraid that my life would be meaningless without him. I discovered that I did not need him. And how wonderful my life became at that moment. At last I had discovered that I had the courage to face what I wanted.

I wanted him to fade.

I did not want to be stuck.

Gloria Gloria had never been stuck in her life — or if so, not for long.

So, in my room that first night home, I called up Gloria.

I began to suppose about this woman whom I had known for no more than two hours, but who now wore some of my clothes and had some of my money and who had admired my children.

I began to suppose where she went when it got too cold and dull to sit in the plaza, to suppose what she did when she got tired of the men honking and whistling.

I called her up. I wrote down what I saw.

A Bed for the Night

Gloria sits for a time under the roof of the open-air building called the Old Slave Market. The breeze from the Matanzas cools her. She is pretty now. Clean. She seems vulnerable, but she is not. She leaves the plaza and crosses Cathedral Street and walks down Charlotte to the Tradewinds. It has been years since she has felt out of place entering a bar alone. She no longer expects heads to turn or any young good-looking men to try their charm on her with a drink before making their passes. But she still smiles at any clever openers, fully prepared to accept, sincerely grateful for almost any man's attentiveness and liberal giving while she makes up her mind to accept or reject his move on her.

She asks for a glass of water at the bar and carries it to an empty table along the wall under a fishnet decorated with glass floats and buoys. She wraps her glass in a cocktail napkin. The first to take her bait is drunk, and she ignores him. The next is young and, on second look at her, veers away mumbling, 'Sorry. I thought you were someone else.'

Her water is almost gone when she looks up at the third, lets their eyes lock, then smiles. That skeptical gaze of hers holds him there. He wears a dark overcoat that is badly stained and buttoned up to his neck. Immediately she feels a pleasant linkage — an electric charge — between them. She nods when he asks if he might sit at her table and nods again when he asks if she would prefer scotch or chablis.

'A glass of scotch to go with this water would be fine,' she says. 'Please.'

It is warm inside the Tradewinds — beads of perspiration glisten on this man's forehead, his hair is straw dry and he smells ever so slightly of bathroom disinfectant, pine oil.

'If I may say so,' he says, 'you appear to have been deposited by someone. Is he coming back?'

'I won't have him if he does.'

'Why then, you have been abandoned. You are a castaway.'

'You could say that. Yes.'

'Gentle breath,' he says, as he raises his glass to her, 'yours my sails must fill or else my project fails, which was to please.' He sips. 'As you from crimes would pardon'd be, let your indulgence set me free!'

Gloria laughs. Her laughter is light, almost like ringing crystal.

So much for openers.

She hasn't realized until that moment that he carries a briefcase with him, which he places on a chair. He gives no indication that he intends to remove or even to unbutton his dark overcoat.

'I am Tromone,' says the man. 'W.B.D. Tromone. That was the epilogue spoken by Prospero, a man — a character — I admire. *The Tempest* is in performance at the Monson Dinner Theater and Motel, where I have engaged a room. I take it you are familiar with the play?'

Tromone smiles, his dark eyes swimming.

'Why don't you take off your coat?' Gloria asks.

' 'Tis best left on,' he says, 'for beneath I am as I was born.' His fingers are wet and delicate — somehow not quite alive — thumb and forefinger badly stained. 'I feel as if I should know you,' he says, smoking his cigarette in a peculiar manner. His lips, which are extraordinarily fleshy, like rubber tubes, have a tendency to stick together as if his saliva were glue, making speech difficult. A man dying of thirst might speak in such a manner, physically. 'I know,' he says, 'Theater Arts, University of Florida, seven years past. I do not forget my students. You were one of the good ones. I recall your performance of Miranda. I believe your husband helped you with the role.'

'You have me confused with someone else,' she says. 'I never finished high school. But,' she adds quickly, 'I've always wanted to be an actress.'

'Is it possible that you don't remember me?' Tromone's eyes are a sad dark brown and his lashes are moist from sentiment.

'Well, maybe I do.' He is gradually becoming familiar to Gloria, who has no memory for faces or names or places, not because she doesn't care, but because there have been so many names and faces in her life thus far, too many to try to remember all of them. So, she is gradually coming to decide that she might remember him after all, this odd, overcoated man. 'Just maybe I do,' she says.

'Let me refresh your memory.'

He signals to the waitress for more drinks and, from his briefcase, removes a volume of the *World Book* encyclopedia. The spine reads: 'Trounce *to* Venial Sin.' He hands the volume to Gloria.

'This is an advance copy,' he says. 'They won't ship it for six weeks. Take a look between "Trolls" and "Trumpet." ' '

The volume falls open to the page and there he is.

'I found you! Is that really you?'

He nods. 'Do take this opportunity to read about me.'

And Gloria does so.

After she finishes, she raises her glass in a half-toast to this famous man who is now slumped in his chair next to her. She doesn't know what else to do. 'I've never met anybody so famous before,' she says.

'Certainly the report is fair and balanced,' Tromone says. 'I wish they had mentioned the children.'

'But,' Gloria says, 'why do they have you dead? They have you dead. You're not dead.' She points to the date on the page. 'March 30. That's in two weeks. See?'

'Of course, I see, dear child. This is an advance copy. It has not been made official. By the time it is being sold door to door across the nation, what it says will no doubt be true.' He shakes his head. 'It would have pleased me if they had included that I hold the time-in-flight record for hang gliding. Of course, to have one's death foretold makes one's spirit shrink just a little, I might say.' He takes a large swallow of scotch. 'They might have mentioned that I breed Golden Retrievers.'

'Have you tried to correct it? Why don't you call them? You've got to make them change it.'

By now Gloria is quite certain she has known this man in her past, and that in her past they were marvelously intimate beyond her dreams and that glory, love, salvation and fulfill-ment are so to be hers. This time it is Gloria who signals the waitress for more to drink.

'You must do something. I care. I remember you now.'

Admittedly, what she feels is strange, but it is true. She does care about this man.

'But I am doing something, dear one. I have taken a room and will remain in this room until after March thirtieth. Then I will file suit against the publishers and create such notice that all my plays, *Nuts, Convalescence, Diet,* all of them, will be called back into print and be trooped across every stage of every high school auditorium in this country.'

'That sounds like a good start. As long as you don't get into an accident before then. Let's finish these drinks and get somewhere safe. What about your room?'

At the door to the Tradewinds, Tromone examines himself in the mirror by the coat rack. 'Those are pearls that were his eyes,' he says. 'Nothing of him that doth fade, but doth suffer a sea change into something rich and strange.'

She takes his arm.

'Watch out for the traffic. I have to make it to the thirtieth.'

'Don't be so morbid. I'll take care of you. Come along. I need a shower before I sleep with you. Come with me, Professor.'

Gloria is pleased with herself for bouncing back so quickly, for finding a man — and a famous one at that — so easily, one who is relatively harmless and who has a bed for her — one night or maybe two nights or maybe weeks. Luck holds. It holds if you let it work for you.

They walk arm in arm along the bay. A few boats are anchored in the harbor. There are a few more nested south of the city pier below the Bridge of Lions.

Tromone mumbles as they stroll. 'I always stay at the Monson. I always have. I like theater while I eat. They're running *Streetcar* after *The Tempest*. I hope I'm still here for it.'

'I suppose she's gone home by now,' says Gloria.

'Who?'

'Meridith Poole, that encyclopedia lady who wrote about your death. I have half a mind to call up the bitch. You're too sweet a man to die just now.'

'She's gone home. It's dark in New York City. Nothing but darkness and death all up the Atlantic seaboard. Full fathom five, soon I shall lie.'

'I forbid you to talk like that.'

She holds his arm tightly and leans on him. They both are rather unsteady, like the ships rolling at anchor in the harbor.

Suddenly she stops them and looks at him full in the face. 'Now I know who you are. I remember you, Professor Tromone. You licked whipping cream from my navel.'

She touches his lips. The skeptical look in her eyes has vanished now. Her eyes are soft on him and warm.

'Remember? We were in your office. You had a basket of strawberries on your desk and a can of Reddi Wip. Remember, Professor Tromone, remember the whipped cream, the fresh ripe strawberries?'

He steers her away from the spotlight in front of the motel's office and away from the outside bar. 'We're in twenty-six,' he replies.

His voice rumbles through her and she snuggles against his shoulder.

'Oh, I remember everything now. Oh yes, I remember everything. It's clear to me now.'

'Don't you have a suitcase or a purse or a backpack or something?'

'Not at the moment,' she says.

She leans against him as he fumbles for the key. The lights are still on in the swimming pool where two mallard ducks, one old and one young, huddle in the deep end under the stubby diving board; they grumble as Tromone grumbles now, trying to work the key. Gloria reaches around this man who smells of scotch whiskey and unlocks the door.

'It's a mess, I'm afraid,' he says. 'I'm working on a project with poultry feathers and have instructed the maids not to vacuum.'

She pushes open the door to twenty-six.

'What I want right now more than anything is a shower,' she says.

The light is on in the bathroom, and Gloria sees that a white layer, which looks at first to be carpet covering, chair covering, bed covering, is sheathing the room in white. The night table, bureau top, television are shimmering with feathers that seem to hover just above the surfaces, that threaten any moment to rise.

Gloria hesitates for a moment before she shuffles across the carpet to the bathroom. Feathers, white pigeon, goose, and chicken feathers, swirl about her ankles.

'Don't they clog the drains?'

'I don't work in the bathroom,' says Tromone.

Tromone sits on the bed. He watches the settling occur about him. He can feel himself gathering strength to leave this world, to glide across the Matanzas River and lift in a slow gyre above Anastasia Island. He can see himself release the ballast in his pockets — his keys and wallet — as a balloonist does and feels himself rise above sea oats and dunes on the southeast wind.

'There are feathers stuck to the mirror in here,' Gloria announces from the bathroom. The shower curtain rattles closed.

Thermals. He will rely on thermals. A steady breeze, an elevation of fifteen hundred feet, the thermals will hold him aloft and will cushion him until he starves to death. He is not a man to jump or gas himself. He will ride the thermals, float east on them as if they were a pile of down pillows.

'God, that felt good. I'm a new person,' she says. 'Do you have a robe?'

Tromone comes out of his thoughts and looks at her.

'I hold time-in-flight records for the hang glider,' he says. 'You are gorgeous, resplendent! Don't put on a robe.'

'Well, move over. Let me get under the covers and out of these feathers. God, I hope I'm not allergic.'

Tromone removes his shoes and socks, then his overcoat. She looks at his naked body.

'You're in good shape.'

'I have to be.'

'What are you doing with a room full of feathers?'

He tells her.

Then he showers and shows her the wing sketches.

'So,' says Gloria, 'you actually plan to get up there on those things and stay up?' She tosses her head. 'I mean, just float around in the clouds and stuff?'

His ankles are ringed with wet feathers.

'Just that.'

Then he looks at her, at her small firm breasts and her legs and the curve of her hip.

'My dear girl,' he says, 'how do you earn your living?'

'What do you think I am?'

'What do you do?'

'I'm in produce,' Gloria says. 'Cabbages actually, until recently that is.'

'I'm in aerodynamics. Free flight, actually. I have left my wife, my hearth, and my home, to pursue this matter in earnest.'

'The guy I was with last left me with our produce business,' she says. 'Right now I'm seeking alternatives.'

'You might try acting,' he says. 'Me, I'm in the middle of a divorce. Quite frankly, it has me unhinged. I'm not entirely committed to these wings. That is, I'm not entirely suicidal, if that's what you're worried about. I'm still open to alternatives. At least I hope I am.'

He swivels to sit cross-legged in front of her. She begins to pick feathers off his ankles. They stick to her fingers. He takes one from her.

'When you arrange these into an efficient form,' he says, 'they have amazing force. Even singularly they are quite powerful.'

He traces the curve of her breast.

'I never thought of feathers as strong or forceful or powerful,' she says, yawning.

The day has caught up with her; she is oblivious now to this lonely man's urgency; she lets her eyes take on a sort of glazed, religious, sensuous look.

'I bet you are a tigress,' he whispers.

She takes him in her hands.

'Yes,' she says. 'I am.'

*

It was mid-morning that Saturday before I got out of bed. Gloria hovered in my thoughts like Spanish moss. I heard my father and his girl friend in the kitchen and went down for coffee.

'We've been up for hours,' Father said, kissing me. He wore a bathing suit and sandals.

His woman was only a few years older than me, with straight straw blond hair. She wore tight pink shorts and a white tank top and had sharp, angular features. At first I thought she was a cheerleader, but her eyes hid an old wound.

'We ate,' she said. 'There are donuts this morning.'

'Don't be fooled by Lee Ann,' my father said. 'During the week she is a lawyer, one of the best.'

Lee Ann laughed. 'Ben, aren't you going to introduce us?'

She is so unlike my soft plump mother, so much more vital. No wonder my father is so youthful these days.

'I want to meet your boys. Are they still sleeping?' she asked.

'I doubt it. What day is it? Saturday. No. They'll be watching cartoons. Every kid in America watches cartoons on Saturday morning. I could use some coffee.'

'First, let's go say good morning to the boys. I won't disturb them.'

I liked this woman immediately. She wasn't the dry and greedy woman I had expected. We looked into the boys' room. Neither Tom nor Alan were aware of us watching them.

'How long are you here for?' Lee Ann whispered.

'I'm not sure. You don't have to whisper. They don't even realize we are here.'

On our way back through the house to the kitchen, I asked, 'Are you living here with him?'

'Off and on, yes. For the last few weeks. I still keep my condo at the beach. Sometimes we stay out there.'

'I hope we're not in your way here.'

'Don't be silly. This house was built to hold a lot of. . .'

'Love,' I said.

Lee Ann, as if she were the woman of the house — and in a way she is — led the way. 'You do understand,' she said. 'I'm not chasing after your father. I can take care of myself. I just happen to be in love with him.'

'Truce,' I said. 'You must be doing something right. He looks better than he has in years.'

At first glance Lee Ann is what I call a Florida girl — her skin is always tanned to the point that the downy hairs on her arms and thighs glisten, from behind her figure is that of a slender boy's. She can make herself look eighteen and yet is a full partner at Bailey, Miller and Selsor, specializing in criminal cases because wills and taxes bore her.

'I can't help what I do for him,' she said, smiling. 'He certainly does something for me.'

'Let's get that coffee,' I said. 'I was up late.'

We sat in the kitchen for a while; then I took a second cup to my room. I wasn't able to concentrate at my desk. A shower helped. I was dressing when the children came in, cranky — sleepy-eyed after a morning of cartoons and cereal ads — and anxious for lunch.

My father had not returned from his golf game with Uncle Jack, so Lee Ann and I ate lunch without him. At first she seems cold. That's because she's shy. She is not as calloused as many other women lawyers I know. Her questions are direct, but not cruel. After the children were fed, we carried our wine glasses outside to the patio facing the river in the sun. The land breeze from the southwest was warm and carried with it the faint scent of the roses, Mother's roses, blooming along the sunny side of the house. There were hints of sea smells in the air that afternoon, an occasional acid and salt odor from the oyster clumps surrounding the dock pilings, marsh grass, when the breeze varied — most of all the air was fresh cut grass, earth and roses.

At some point during lunch Lee Ann asked, 'What about your husband? You must miss him in a way, at least.'

'I'm not sure. I guess I'm still in shock.'

'What will you do here? What do you have to do?'

I gazed at Lee Ann's shoes and was silent for a time. They were flip-flops and belonged on the feet of a teenager. It wasn't simply a matter of finding something to do or having something to do to keep myself occupied, to keep my mind off things. It was a matter of finding the courage to face myself and to begin to act for myself.

'It's difficult to explain,' I said to her. 'In a way, I am searching for a missing person, an abandoned person. I'm trying to find the person I gave up when I married Arthur.'

One of Lee Ann's flip-flops came loose from her foot and dropped onto the patio.

'A search?' she asked. 'You are trying to find yourself?'

'I suppose. You see, I came across this story of a young woman who was taken to an island and left there for months on end. It struck a chord in me. I've been there. I've lived the kind of life that woman lived. I have pretended I was she and know how she felt. What was going on around her. What happened. That woman was really abandoned — more than I was when Mother died, more than when Arthur would go off and leave the kids and me in the trailer. This woman didn't even have a canoe. I wanted to know how she felt being left that way. Now I do.'

'Why did you put yourself through that misery?' She ran her fingers through her blond hair.

'I wasn't sure at first. I think I am now. By understanding her situation I am able, or was able, to understand my own, to see it clearly. When you are caught up in something like mine it is hard to get a perspective. I'm not as strong a person as I'd like to be,' I told her.

Lee Ann listened attentively and with sympathy. I understood even more clearly why my father felt such affection for her.

'There were times,' I told her, 'when I could feel this woman inside me. That may sound crazy, but I know her. We could talk to each other. You'd probably call her an imaginary friend. But she was more than that, Lee Ann. She gave me the courage to leave him. No one else did. When I saw how much alike our lives were, I couldn't take it. I didn't want to wind up as she did. I didn't want to be stuck like her. Oh, I'm probably not making any sense.'

'Did your husband beat you or hurt you?' she asked.

'No. He ignored me, is all. He would go off for days and days with other women and leave us. The only reason we were living in that trailer is Arthur likes to live there. We could have bought a house with my money, but he wouldn't have that. So we lived in the trailer and he would go away, just as her husband went away. And I got to know her because our condition was the same — we were abandoned, and we waited. Then, I realized that I had to go on living whether he was there or not. So I left him.'

I found it easy to talk to Lee Ann. She did not seem to judge me.

'I took it for as long as I could. Sometimes it was all right. And it actually was, sometimes. I suppose I could have stuck it out. But I felt dead inside. Now I feel awake, but I'm a little frightened.'

'And you could actually talk with her and you know what she looks like?' Lee Ann asked without criticism.

'Very clearly.' Then I began to cry. 'I'm sorry. I guess I'm more upset than I thought I was.'

She was silent for a while, then she asked, 'Did you have any lovers when you were with him?'

I felt myself go tight inside, my stomach clenched.

'Sorry. I shouldn't have asked that,' she said.

'No. That's all right. There was almost one. He is an archaeologist. He spent the night with me once, but we weren't lovers. I wanted to be, but I still hoped that Arthur and I would get back together — I couldn't do it. I thought I still loved him. Now I wish I had had that lover. At least he was interested in me. I mean interested in what I was doing there. He would arrive early in the morning and go into the woods, then he would have lunch with me and we would listen to music. We didn't talk that much. We didn't need to. We sat outside and listened to music and looked at the river. I probably should have made love with him. We wanted to, but he was free and I wasn't.'

'You are now,' Lee Ann said. 'Find an excuse to see him.'

'Maybe I'll try to find him.'

I knew perfectly well that I was able and free to find him, but something was holding me back. For now.

'It does take time after all,' she said. 'Believe me, it takes time. I was off men — totally celibate — for nearly eight months after my first husband.'

I understood Lee Ann's silence.

Finally, she said, 'I was incapacitated for the first month. Worse than you are. Then I could crawl. After about a year, I was myself. I mean, I became a new self. I was divorced for three and a half years before I fell in love with your father. You know, I couldn't have fallen in love, not even with him, before then. Too many ghosts. Sure I went out with men, but I wasn't really with them. I can't even remember what happened to me. I just know that the first three weeks after my husband and I broke up were the hardest. I was scattered and scared and lost and ungrounded. No matter how smart you are, or what you have to draw from, or how safe you are. . .'

The afternoon wore on and we moved from the patio across the sun-flooded lawn to the dock where we sat next to one another looking out at the still river letting our feet swing inches above the water. The *Miranda* bobbed gently on the ripples.

Lee Ann asked me to tell her more about the woman on the island.

'Her name is Sallie Stevens,' I said. 'Sometimes she is as real as a friend. I've studied the time she lived in, I've actually lived where she lived, I know about her family. When you do that, the person becomes real, as real as the people you know. The same thing happens to people who write biographies. They feel genuine grief when their subject dies. At times I have believed that Sallie Stevens is my sister.'

Lee Ann gathered her flip-flops and stood. I had been so busy talking that I didn't notice my father and Uncle Jack pull into the driveway. I didn't want to see Uncle Jack.

Lee Ann waved to my father.

'I don't want to see them.'

'You go inside,' she said. 'I'll head them off.'

A few minutes later I heard Uncle Jack's car leave, and my father began to make noises about taking everyone out for a sail on the *Miranda*.

He found me in the kitchen.

'What do you think?'

'About what?'

'Lee Ann? What's my daughter's verdict?'

'Oh. We've had a nice time together. But Daddy, I don't feel like going for a sail. She's awfully nice, Lee Ann is. And I like her,' I said, trying to hide my puffy face from him. 'I really do.'

I helped the boys with their life jackets and stood on the dock helping with the lines, waiting for them to go, grateful to be able to return inside.

Then from the window of my room, I watched the *Miranda* tack down river and head toward the inlet. The tide was out, exposing the granite dock piers and oyster shell clumps, which cut deep wounds that heal slowly.

I lay on my bed for a while and thought of Arthur — pushed him away — thought of my father — pushed him away — and finally let into my thoughts the strange man, who was not unlike my husband in a certain way, but who did not look at all like my husband. I saw Gloria first, then the man whom Gloria called Tromone. He was lying naked — as I was — on his back.

My notebook was on the bedside table.

After a time, I began to write down what I saw.

Ride on my Back

Tromone is covered with feathers. He is taking his good slow mid-day time picking feathers off Gloria's small breasts and her neck and shoulders. Soon she begins to work on him.

'Don't bother with the armpits,' Tromone sighs, as he uses a long pin feather to caress one nipple, then the other, with such delicacy that Gloria stops her own labors to lie with arms outstretched and to move slightly, undulating under his touch as if she were floating on her back in the lukewarm sea. She can hear his voice and tries to ignore it.

'Ours is a pragmatic age,' Tromone says to her. 'We all seek what we can gain from our actions. Even our acts of altruism are not perceived as selfless acts. There are no true altruistic acts in our time. I do this to you knowing I will get something from you in return. You receive this from me knowing you will return, must return, something to me. I give you roses, you give me love.'

'Oh, shut up, Tromone,' Gloria whispers. 'Shut up for once. I don't care why you're doing what you're doing.' She moans now at his touch. 'Just don't stop. Don't stop.'

His hands begin to move over her, and he is reminded of a young cat purring. The cat is starving for human touch, but extends her claws rather than retracts them when petted as Tromone pets Gloria now. And Gloria is the same when she feels pleasure; her nails go to work on Tromone. She seems to want to wound this man.

'Be gentle,' he whispers. 'Don't draw blood.'

The picking of feathers becomes for them a delicious and endless task. Every turn upon the mattress, every shift of position causes more of them to adhere to her skin and more to his.

Then Tromone becomes methodical and continues to work the same basic spots, the ones which give Gloria pleasure. As he works these isolated areas she does not complain.

'They gather here,' Tromone says, 'and here and here.'

When he blows away a downy breast feather, she can feel the warmth, a rush of pleasure runs from tailbone to skull.

'Here and here and here,' she says, echoing him, removing them from his cock so her lips will not become infested with their dryness, their cloying. She is fastidious about this removal for she does not like them on her lips. And then she takes his cock into her mouth to use lips and tongue.

She rolls over and over for him.

Tromone holds her breasts.

'Oh, Tromone,' says Gloria, 'I do like you.'

Her heart cannot sing to him. It cannot sing.

She cannot say, 'I love you.'

'She likes me,' says Tromone, grinning like a boy. 'She likes me.'

'This is the first time for me with feathers,' says Gloria. She has retreated into herself now, recharging her batteries. She is herself again.

'I find them very interesting,' says Tromone.

He moves to the closet and exposes a green athletic locker which is secured with a combination lock. He taps the locker. The door flies open.

'What we have here,' he says, lifting out a pair of wing frames partially covered with feathers, 'is my last project. I will use the driveway in front of the Monson Dinner Theater and Motel as my runway. I will use my fierce faith in my own self esteem as my only fuel. I will soar!'

The sperm on her belly attracts a cluster of down.

'I want to be your last project,' she says softly. 'I like you, Tromone.'

'If it pleases you, you may ride on my back.'

He slips on the wing frame as if he were hefting a backpack.

'Imagine our flight. We will soar above the petty world, rise above the wretched landscape upon which we conduct our meaningless and absurd lives.'

She sneezes. A cloud of feathers rises from her breasts and settles between her legs.

'What if you kill yourself? What about your wife? Don't you have children who love you? They will be ashamed to go on living.'

'Oh, it's up, up for me!'

He arranges a pair of white shoes, white swim trunks, white helmet and goggles on the bed.

'I'll leave no trace. No bloody mess,' says he.

It isn't until that moment, with Tromone fully erect again — his thighs and belly covered with feathers — that Gloria realizes Tromone does intend to kill himself.

'Of course, we'll get a flying outfit for you.'

He looks at her from behind his eyes. His appearance is cheerful and bright on the surface, engaging in a crazy sort of way that appeals to her enormously. He is like a practical, puckish, pipe–smoking elf with wings and an enormous erection; but behind that she sees such a lust that her heart threatens to ignite into flames. She cannot allow that deep fire to fall into the sea. Such a waste!

'Come here,' she says.

Tromone moves toward her. His wrists are hooked in leather straps at the wing tips. He raises and lowers his arms, knocking over a standing lamp. She opens her arms to him and sees only white. Then she feels the bed give and looks up at a gigantic figure — proud, poised, erect with quivering silver wing tips.

'God, you are beautiful, Tromone! I have never seen anything more beautiful.'

The wings move through the swirling whiteness, and she pulls him on to her and in her passion cries out for him.

'Don't fly away on those! You'll kill yourself!'

She opens her legs.

'Here, Tromone. Kill me! Kill me here!'

Then he bellows to some unknown god within, pleading for strength, for firmness, for warmth. Then, suddenly, as if to obey his prayer — their prayer — the room begins to spin; and with his lips pressed against hers, there begins the warm, familiar, steady rhythm which they both can comprehend.

*

The window curtains blew over my face then. At first it felt like the beating of wings, then like flight, and soon I lost myself in a swirl and tumble of falling and rising sparked with silver light.

I must have slept.

Next I heard a knocking and rolled onto my stomach.

'Mom? Are you in there? Are you awake?'

I didn't know which one of them it was at first.

'Alan?'

'It's me. It's Tom. We're supposed to have dinner now. Grandfather wants you to come down.'

I covered my naked body.

'I'll be there in a minute, darling. I'm writing. How was your sail?'

'Fun. Grandfather went out to get chicken from the Colonel. Lee Ann is making broccoli with cheese. Come on.'

'I'll be down.'

'Are you sick?'

'I'm sleepy, is all.'

Tom opened the door and stood beside the bed.

'You're all sweaty. Your face is red.'

'That's enough, Tom. I'll be down in a minute.'

'Do we have to wait for you?' He got on the bed.

'No. You don't have to wait for me. Now, leave me alone for a minute. Please. I'd like to get dressed.'

He hopped off the bed and ran out of the room. His voice echoed in the stairwell, broadcasting to everyone within ear-shot that his mother was red-faced, sweaty and naked on her bed, but that she would be downstairs for dinner in a minute.

On Palm Sunday morning Water Street was quiet. Earlier I had heard my father and Lee Ann leave for church. I was at my desk writing. Outside the trees and houses were tented with a layer of marsh fog. I saw the uniformed man from the flower shop park his truck a few houses down and make his way across the Manucys' and the Paltings' front lawn, reading house numbers. He wore wire-framed glasses with circular rims and carried the long white box in his arms as if it were a child's coffin. I went downstairs and met him on the path in front of the house. The box held a dozen beautiful long-stemmed red roses.

I love roses. A surge of anger outstripped my initial delight. The nerve of that man! He must be told never to send me roses again! He must be told. I will always accept roses. I will never send them back to the flower shop. That would be impossible, as impossible as it is to replant them, to reattach them to their stems.

Yes.

I must accept roses.

Always.

As I suspected, the card read: 'From your husband, love Arthur.'

The delivery man stood nearby waiting.

I had been up most of the night and must have looked like a wraith in my pink bathrobe.

'I'm sorry,' said the delivery man. 'You have my sympathy.'

'Thank you. But no one has died. They're from my husband.'

'Oh,' he said. 'I am sorry.'

I moved off the sidewalk and stood on the dew–covered grass and proceeded then to make a thorough ass of myself.

'That's all right,' I said to the young man. 'We were trying to destroy each other anyway.'

I approached him. He was a few years younger than I am.

'Something went wrong,' I told him. 'It shouldn't hurt so much.'

'No. It shouldn't. I like delivering flowers. They make people feel better. Even if they are sad it makes people feel better to get flowers. Especially roses.' He started to back away from me.

Tears came to my eyes. 'I'm sorry. I know I'm not supposed to do this. But he shouldn't have sent them. I had to leave him. I couldn't take it any longer. And now he does this. It's cruel. It is. Don't you think so? It's insensitive.'

'The order said specifically to deliver them this morning,' he said. 'I wouldn't be here otherwise.' Then a flood of tears came. I cried until rage overtook remorse: the recent blasts of his shotgun, his language, his abuse, the senseless damage to my home, all helped to drive out self-pity.

'I am sorry,' I said. 'I'm not normally like this.'

'Please,' he said, 'will you sign here.'

'I don't want these,' I said. 'I really don't. They are my favorite. I hate him right now.' I gave him back his ball point.

As he walked toward his truck, I held out the box of flowers as if they would fly to him. They didn't. They did not leave my arms and sail across the yard to the delivery van. So I walked back to the house carrying the flowers the way the delivery man had — as if I were carrying a child's coffin.

I couldn't leave them on the kitchen table, so I trimmed the stems slightly and put them in one of Mother's vases. The light through the kitchen window made the dew on the leaves sparkle. Their fragrance followed me upstairs.

On my bed I clutched my pillow. Helplessness. Hate. Shame.

Arthur's selfishness, his cold lack of consideration, his unconsciousness of his own being, his wanting it both ways, infuriated me. That's what makes him so evil, I realized, truly evil. He sent me something beautiful knowing it would hurt.

The telephone rang. I let it.

After a time, I heard the car on the crushed oyster shells of the driveway. Their voices in the kitchen exclaimed over the roses.

The telephone rang again.

My father called my name.

I did not answer him.

After a while he knocked. 'I brought you some coffee,' he said, opening my door. He brought the steaming mug to me. 'I see an admirer of yours has sent you flowers.'

I sat up and stuffed my pillow behind me. 'That was very cruel of him.'

'I don't want to interfere.'

I huddled around the mug of coffee letting the steam rise to my face.

'But I would like to tell you something.'

I nodded. Nothing he could say would help.

'After your mother died,' he said, 'I went back to a woman I had been in love with years before I fell in love with your mother. I didn't know why I did that, at the time. It was so soon after her death. I kept it a secret from you. I was ashamed and felt disloyal to her memory.'

My father looked tired.

'Daddy, are you sure you want to tell me about this?'

As if he had a speech prepared, Father continued: 'Now I know why I went back to her. And I think she does too. I went back to her to finish something — to complete what I had left unfinished long ago when I fell in love with your mother and married her. This woman and I stayed together as long as we needed to — until we both agreed that we had ended it between us. It took almost a year and a half. We stopped without a wrenching apart. We didn't cause each other any pain. We will always love each other, I'm sure of that, as true friends.'

'You want me to go back to Arthur, don't you? You're trying to talk me into it. I could never be friends with Arthur — it wasn't like that with us.'

'No, honey. All I want is to make certain that you understand that loves, marriages, friendships, all end best if you can, somehow, let them come to their own conclusion at their own rate of speed in their own time.

'Remember that your mother's death was sudden and unexpected. She and I were far from finished, as far as I was concerned. I resented her killing herself, her leaving me . . . us. I did feel left, abandoned by her suicide. As I understand myself now, I went back to this woman — I'm not going to tell you who she is because you know her — I went back to her to end a passionate romance and to create a friendship. We ended our romance without surprise or shock or cruelty; we transformed it into a friendship with grace.'

'But I don't want to be friends with Arthur,' I said firmly. 'He's not right for me. I want to be rid of him for good and to get on with my own life. That's what I want. We could never be friends.'

'Is there someone else, then?' he asked. 'Another man? There usually is.'

'No. Don't be silly.'

'Are you certain?'

'Of course, I'm certain.' Sometimes my father makes me angry. 'You would know if there was.'

'Then, Arthur. He must still feel something for you. I take it those flowers in the kitchen are from him.'

'I should have smashed those roses! It was cruel of him to send them!'

I could not stop the cold resentment. Hard, cold, solitary. I was without him now; he was crazy. He had seemed so casual when I last saw him, stalking off into the woods leaving us all behind, opening his hands that way, letting his little injured bird go free. Evil. Selfish. Calloused. Inhuman. I felt a pressure on my chest.

Then Father spoke as if he were singing some sort of a song, one he had sung to himself many times. I could not look at him. I closed my eyes and tried to recapture the nothing of a few minutes before, struggled, barely hearing him as if his voice were coming to me in a dream. I leaned back against my pillow, and his voice soothed me. The trance, the nothing did return. I was half sleeping, but could hear my father's voice — his song. The old feeling of the house, empty and closed, came back to me. But it was different now. There was no sadness in my father's voice nor in the feelings it provoked in me. His voice held me there in half-sleep, then gradually I felt myself coming awake.

'I use only a small portion of this house, even now,' he said. 'The den, where she and I spent our last hours together. At first, I was lost without her. The house was too big for me, so I lived in a corner of it. Probably, I should have left. After all, my mother built this house to entertain in — it was built to be used. It was built for love, not gloom, not solitude. Just as my mother wanted the Fountain of Youth to be a place for lovers to use, she wanted this house to be full of love. I became blind to the spirit of this house, blind to the spirit of restoration and hope symbolized by the Fountain of Youth. That's why I let my brother Jack run the fountain. Why I kept the house closed. I must sound like one of the converted. I am.

'Night after night, I used to sit alone in the evening and listen to Bach. Hour after hour. I am not certain why, except he is the one composer I can tolerate. Gradually, I educated myself to the fact that one day I, too, will die. If anything, your mother's death put me on that path toward understanding. I was afraid. I was bitter. I was empty. Bach makes it easier, somehow, to accept life.

'Then, grief left me. After a certain length of time, grief becomes morbid and sentimental. If you don't accept dying as a part of life, you become bitter and helpless in the face of death. Death is inevitable. Accept that. Endings are inevitable. The only alternative to acceptance is bitterness. And there can be joy in acceptance.

'I found beauty in Bach. Certainly not sentimentality. He is stable and sure and fulfilling. The force of his music is a redemptive force. His music comforts me; I am restored. But my resignation, or whatever you want to call it, did not happen quickly. At times I thought that I would keep this house closed up for ever. At times I felt I was riding a glacier — slow and cold and massively lonely. A mass of despair.

'One composition moves me more than the others, I don't know why. It is not long, not complicated — beautiful in structure, and swift. "Wachet Auf" it's called, "Sleepers Awake".

'I listen to it over and over. Now, when I listen to it, I see a lone woman on a park bench waving to her husband who is moving away. He wears black. He can't stop moving away. She can't leave the bench. At first he thinks about her. As the distance widens between them, he begins to think about himself. Her time in the world is over. He must continue. The music begins with the trumpet's melody with the strings in the background. Gradually the trumpet fades and the strings take over. When I first began to listen to the piece, I mourned the fading trumpet for it was so clear and strong. Then I understood something. The music is so beautiful because the trumpet's strength does fade into silence. It must happen. The trumpets must fade.'

My father finished his song. He sat on my bed waiting.

I opened my eyes and looked at him then, as if for the first time.

'I've never heard you talk like that before,' I said. 'Why didn't I know this side of you before? Dear God, how I needed you this way.'

'I wasn't able,' he said.

We both were quiet for a time. I had to tell him.

'But, Daddy, it's not the same as it was with Mother or that woman you loved before. Arthur didn't die. He has never been my friend. He hurt me. I can't respect him. I don't trust him. Don't you see? I don't think I even like him any more.'

'Not even one last try?'

'You don't understand. I have tried. I'm worn out trying.'

'He wants to try. He wants to see you.'

I felt my skin sting. A rush of panic went through me. 'He's not here. No! Is he?'

'That was Arthur on the phone. Didn't you hear it?'

'What did you tell him?'

'Well, I left it that you would call when you felt you were ready.'

'And what did he say to that?'

'Honey, he wanted to know if I think you will come back to him.'

I shook my head.

'So, I told him that I don't know. I said that I thought you were too deeply hurt just now. After all, you've hardly left this room since you got here. I don't think you want to see anyone just now. Certainly not him. I do understand. I'm not pushing you.'

'I know. I'll be fine. I just need time alone right now. You know me. When I get hurt I withdraw.'

He stood.

'There's someone else I know who does that,' he said.

'Thanks, Daddy. I mean thanks for telling me about . . . everything . . . I'm glad you told him what you did. All I know now is he can't hurt me any more than he has already. I let him do that to me — that's what hurts. I let him do it to me over and over and over. I have to get over my shame about that, too.'

My father closed the door to my room and I heard him go down the hall toward the guest room where the boys were.

I was much better after that talk with my father. He had seldom shown such understanding.

When I looked at the draft of my dissertation that morning, it seemed dead to me. Cold. Academic. I tried to call up Sallie Stevens, but she didn't come. Busy waiting. She was busy being stuck, I decided. I left her alone. My notes all made sense. I was prepared to describe the demographics of East Florida during the second Spanish occupation, using the statistics I had drawn from my search in the records and the

individuals — Sallie Stevens among them — for my examples
and case studies. But I continued to be drawn more toward
my writing about Gloria. So, for the first time since I married
Arthur, I followed my own inclinations and no one else's.

I didn't write my letter withdrawing from the anthropology
department at the university that day, but I began to seriously
consider it that afternoon. I was in the middle of describing
Gloria cleaning the feathers off her in Tromone's motel room,
when Lee Ann tapped on my door looking for my father who
was down the hall with the boys.

'Ben?' Lee Ann whispered. 'Are you in there?'

'There's no one here but us recluses,' I said.

'I hope I'm not interrupting, but your uncle is here.
Actually, he says he's here to see you.'

'I suppose I should at least say hello.'

'What's the trouble? He doesn't seem that bad to me.'

'I've got to get dressed.'

'You look fine.'

'Not for Uncle Jack, I don't.'

I put on a pair of baggy jeans and a big shirt. Lee Ann
checked herself in the mirror. She wore the same pink top and
short white shorts and looked, as before, healthy and sexy.

'Every time I'm near him,' I told her, 'I feel as if his eyes
have fingers.'

'You mean he does that to you, too? You're his niece.'

I didn't tell Lee Ann that I have avoided my uncle since I
was fifteen and try never to be alone with him. He was the first
male to put his hands on my breasts and between my legs. I
had allowed him to do that — one time. I have been ashamed
of myself ever since. When I am with him, I have the feeling
that he wants to finish what he started with me more than ten
years ago. He isn't a repulsive man and I suppose I am a little
afraid of him because there have been times when I have
thought about it.

Uncle Jack was on the couch in the living room. He is not
fat, but massive in his silver leisure suit. Imposing. His skin is

leather from hours on the golf course and his neck is thick. My
uncle likes to pretend he's the redneck that my husband likes
to pretend he isn't. Though Uncle Jack eats and drinks too
much, he is healthy, powerful and proud. That day he wore
his official cap — a gold baseball cap with five stars on the
crown and the words 'Fountain of Youth'.

I watched his eyes look me over and knew immediately that
he continues to harass, without the slightest remorse, any
female who has two legs and breasts. I know for certain that
many of the 'Indian Maidens' who work for him as tour
guides cooperate with him on the leather couch in his office —
some to keep their jobs, some because they like it. He is not an
unattractive man. He smiled. The zipper on the front of his
leisure suit looked like well–lubricated teeth. And the crazy
thought came to me: what would Gloria be like around Jack
Phillips; how would Gloria handle my uncle?

'Do you want a job at the Fountain?' he asked.

'I don't need one,' I said. 'Thanks to Grandmother.'

That's true. Even my uncle, with his twisting of history to
jazz up the property, has not stopped the visitors. The family
has been living off the Fountain ever since my grandmother
started it in the early 1900's. Her inventiveness and ability to
maneuver publicity has resulted in the Fountain remaining —
in the mind of the public at least — as the genuine landing
spot of Ponce de Leon on that Easter day (Pascua Florida) in
April, 1513, when he shouted, 'La Florida!' and raised the flag
of Spain upon what is now our family's property, claiming
possession of the land of flowers in the name of his king,
Fernando of Spain. Though no one knows for certain exactly
where on the Atlantic coast Ponce de Leon set foot, my
grandmother's gift for publicity has permanently set the
location where it is today, knocking away all contenders for
the spot from Key West to the mouth of the St Johns River
near the Georgia border. And thanks to my uncle — who
wears his silver metallic leisure suit in memory of Ponce de
Leon's armor, serves 'youth juice' to the tourists, and has as

much of the con artist in him as my grandmother did — the place continues to net enough income every year to maintain the life style of our entire family, including two of Uncle Jack's ex-wives.

'A job would keep you busy,' said my uncle. 'And I could keep my eye on you.'

'You don't want me working there, Uncle Jack. I might tell the tourists the truth.'

He laughed at me. 'You've agreed not to do that — at least not all of it. Besides, if you cause the attendance to drop, you're only hurting yourself.'

I could never cause the attendance to drop. I wouldn't want to anyway. I love the fountain as much as Uncle Jack does — for different reasons. The part of the truth I'd agreed not to tell in my master's thesis was how the property came into the family in the first place. Some St Johns County Circuit Court cases in the 1900's indicate that my grandmother and grand-father, whom she divorced, might have swindled the property away from the previous owner. Accusations were made. The charges were dropped. I'd promised my uncle to leave that part out of my thesis.

As if to mock me, Uncle Jack turned on the huckster in him: 'What is the Fountain of Youth? Step right up, folks. Let us cast a veil of magic over your eyes. Come sip from the legendary well and be revitalized. Regenerate your hopes. Restore your potency.'

'That's what Grandmother used to advertise,' I said, recalling the early pamphlets she handed out with a cup of water for fifty cents. 'You don't still say that, do you?'

'You'll have to visit.'

'I think I can imagine it perfectly well. I'd rather go there when you're closed. That's when it's the most peaceful. I liked it when I was little and Grandmother had peacocks.'

Uncle Jack smiled at me again. 'You look good, Nancy.' He held out a batch of papers which I hadn't noticed he was carrying. 'I found these in my desk the other day. They're yours.'

I recognized them at once. 'These are my early notes for my master's thesis!'

'I don't know how they wound up with me,' he said. 'I was going through some stuff the other day and they turned up.'

I know how they wound up with him. He had demanded that I give him all of my notes along with my bibliography, so he could approve. Then he pretended to lose them, and I had to promise to leave out the part about the acquiring of the property, or start all over again. I promised, but he never returned my notes.

'Why are you giving this back to me now?'

'I heard about your troubles. I think you're old enough now, you wouldn't do anything to hurt business.'

'You're really something.'

'Now, don't get all disgusted with me, sweetness. I'm just looking after the family business, that's all. You were Miss High-and-Mighty back then, full of Ideals and Truth. You've calmed down some.'

'So you trust me now. Is that it?'

'Sure. Now that you don't need this stuff any more. You got your degree without it. Also, it looks to me like you've matured some.'

'Uncle Jack, I'm not in very good shape right now, and I really don't feel like fighting with you. I think I'll just go and heat up my coffee and see if I can get some work done. I hope you'll understand if I excuse myself.'

'Certainly, sweetness, you just run right along.'

I stormed upstairs and went swiftly to my room, slamming my door. The man is a bastard, a greasy smart-assed bastard! So is Arthur. I hate both of them. I socked my feather pillow.

They really *are* bastards, both of them. My uncle and my husband. They both treat me the same way — the way southern men treat women, for the most part, pretending they are objects — and I didn't know how to make either one of them stop it, and all I could do was to go strange with men the way Grandmother did or give in or run away. I ran away from my uncle and gave in to my husband — but it amounted to the same thing. In the end they were still in control; and I lost control in their presence, which made me act like I wasn't alive, was an object, which is what they wanted in the first place.

The thought of those two made me sick of myself.

I went to my desk and waited, trying to find Gloria. I pushed everything away and waited. Searching for nothing. Gloria would come to me. Relax, I told myself. Gloria Gloria will come. She will teach you how to love.

And soon she did come. And I began once again to write down what I saw.

The Indian Maiden

Gloria has finished filling the pillowcases with feathers and ties off the openings with strips torn from the disposable shoe cloth provided by the management. Feathers grow out of the carpet even now; they are more difficult to pick from the rug than shards of broken glass.

She wears a gray dress — Tromone has bought her this outfit — red shoes, red scarf and red belt. Her fingernails are red. She leaves the room.

Gloria is going to find herself a job.

She walks to a small wooden booth and buys a trailer train ticket — which gives her on and off privileges if she displays the day-glow sticker on her breast — for the sightseeing train that will pass by all of the city's tourist attractions. She boards the rear car and sits facing backwards.

At the International Doll Museum she is told that she will have to dress properly for work each day. She does not have such clothes. The Wax Museum is nice, but the statue of Pedro Menendez de Aviles (the city's founding father) looks too much like Tromone. The massive Castillo de San Marcos is not hiring seasonal help until early summer. She inquires at the Moorish castle on King Street which is built of reinforced concrete and is an imitation of the Alhambra; she inquires at Ripley's 'Believe It or Not' Museum; at the Spanish Quarter where for eight hours a day the guides re-enact the lives of the hard-laboring first Spanish colonial settlers, including chickens, which reminds her too much of life on a cabbage farm at Hastings now in her distant past; she inquires at the Oldest Wooden School House which is held together by a massive anchor chain as if the ghosts of past students press the walls from within, anxious for recess; at the Tragedy Museum where the owner absently polishes the hood ornament of Kennedy's death car; at the Oldest House. There the head tour guide, a short fat woman with an olive complexion and a Spanish name, chirps her way through a tangle of dark rooms crowded with bric-a-brac, trailing her fringed shawl. They stop before the Lord's Prayer which has been cut by a jigsaw from plywood, at Martha Washington's glass-knobbed vanity table, at Napoleon's traveling pillow still plump with goose down and displayed on a canopied oak bed with carved chameleons and armadillos chasing one another up the four posts and across the headboard. 'This is . . . This is . . . This is,' her guide says, pointing from object to object to object, continuing her presentation long after the last glimmering of curiosity and politeness have faded to a glaze in Gloria's eyes. She finds herself surfeited and numb, still nodding at the guide, when they emerge from the old house into the bright sunlight. 'You look so Spanish yourself,' says the guide. 'The job is yours if you want it. We furnish the costumes.' Gloria thanks the woman politely and hurries to catch a passing sightseeing train and swings aboard the last car to be whisked north along the bayfront to the Fountain of Youth.

A man has seen this woman dressed in gray and red walking toward the ticket booth. He unzips his silver leisure suit an inch or two and hires her before she opens her mouth.

'You can start right now,' he says.

She takes the application.

'Listen to the other girls and memorize the speech word for word. Don't change it. You'll do fine. More than that.'

'Do I get a costume?' she asks.

'Locker eight is free. The costume's inside. One size fits all. We like our girls to spill out of them a bit. Try out your talk on one of the other girls first. Always hand out the water after the speech. Not before. Smile. Flirt if you like the looks of a guy. It makes them want to kick up their heels. But don't say nothing more about this place than what's in the speech. They come here wanting a fairy tale. They know it's a fairy tale, so let them pretend for a while. What's the harm? Maybe their old lady's holding out on them. Let them have a dream. They pay for it. Give them what they pay for. A little dream, sweetness. Make the women feel beautiful again. Make the men feel wanted. You look to me like you've done plenty of that. Keep it clean. Keep it innocent. No solicitation. Show a little leg sometimes. Keep a few buttons undone on the front. Let a little spill out. You'll do fine. You keep me happy, I'll keep you happy. Do we understand each other?'

Gloria smiles at the jerk, shy.

'You're awfully kind to let me try, Mr Phillips.'

'Jack,' he says. 'The younger ones call me Uncle Jack. You got a husband?'

'Not at the moment.'

'That's good. Then you're hungry.'

Gloria dresses in the Indian Maiden costume and goes to the well house. She hears the speech once. It sticks.

By noon she is a natural Indian Maiden telling visitors about Ponce de Leon's Fountain of Youth.

With ease and freshness, over and over again, Gloria says to the tourists: Hello, I'm Gloria. Welcome to the Fountain of Youth! Before you leave here today, I want you all to take a sip from our magic spring, our marvelous spring of pure mineral water, which will put new youth in your step and spring where you need it, if not melt away years. (Pause. Smile. Make eye contact.) Do you realize that years before Columbus discovered America there were rumors of this Fountain? You stand on famous ground. Soon you will taste a magic elixir. (Pause. Gesture toward the well.)

On she talks — glib, persuasive, charming. . .

So, good friends, drink!

Drink to youth!

Drink to love!

Then she passes the visitors little white plastic cups. Concluding her speech each time. . . Now, before you taste the water, imagine a seaman like Ponce de Leon. Imagine how the cool clear water from this deep natural spring must have rejuvenated him. We all seek eternal youth. We all wish, as did Ponce de Leon, to look and feel younger than we do. This fountain has inspired the imagination of great men . . . Peter Martyr . . . Gonzalo Oveido . . . Pope Leo the Tenth . . . John Mandeville. (Pause. Gesture. Smile. More eye contact.) Please join me now. Come. Let's sip from Ponce de Leon's Fountain of Youth. Let's drink to his exploration and discovery.

After work, she catches a ride on a sightseeing train which drops her off at the entrance to the Monson Dinner Theater and Motel.

'I have a job,' she tells Tromone.

He helps her remove her new gray dress, but sometime during their celebration in room twenty-six, the telephone rings. Tromone is informed by his lawyer that he must leave for his home to finish his divorce.

'I'll come back,' he says to Gloria. 'I'll be back soon.'

'Don't you leave me stuck here, Tromone. Don't you run off to some other woman while I wait for you. Don't you dare, Tromone. I'll kill you if you do.'

Before they sleep, she takes one of his earlobes into her mouth and sucks. She pierces it with a tooth.

'Now you won't forget me,' she whispers.

And, again in the morning, she stands in the open door to room twenty-six. She is naked.

'Don't forget me, Tromone. Don't forget.'

'I will be back.'

'If you're leaving me, I won't be faithful.'

A sudden wind gust carries off his reply, across the parking lot, across the bay.

Tromone will return. He is not leaving her stuck in the Monson Dinner Theater and Motel. His divorce will take a week's time. He is not abandoning her (as so many others have), they both know that. She just wants to make certain. All she wants just then is someone next to her, someone who is attractive — Tromone is attractive to her — someone who wants to make love with her — Tromone certainly does that. That's all she wants. To make love with someone helps, makes her feel worth something. That's all she wants. All she needs. She has everything else she wants. She had not expected such passion with Tromone. She had thought the fireworks were over for her. Well, they aren't. She has someone she wants. Someone who is kind to her, who loves her for herself. She finally has what makes her life in this world of swamp, flat rotting swamp, lonely dead swamp, worthwhile. But now he's gone. And she is stuck. Damn you, Tromone. Hurry up!

Day after day at the Fountain of Youth the tourists walk away from her. Tourists with cameras and colored hats.

'Thank you for your attention. I hope you enjoy your visit to Saint Augustine,' she says to them.

One afternoon Jack approaches her. He strides up to the well house after the last group of the day.

'Aren't you doing the planetarium show?' she says.

'I was hoping you'd fill my jug,' says Jack, producing a plastic milk carton. He moves toward her, admiring her openly, all the while looking into her eyes, those eyes which seem to tell him that he has arrived at the right moment. 'It's true, you know, this stuff is an aphrodisiac — if you believe it.'

'You're a tease,' she laughs. She raises her cup and sips.

Then, looking at him, she pulls up her skirt slightly and sits on the edge of the well. 'Of course, help yourself.'

Flirt with them, he has told her. Make them feel wanted. She will show him she can flirt. 'Be my guest,' she says, handing him the ladle.

'Do you believe this stuff works?' he asks.

'It must. It pays my bills,' she says.

Then she gives him her skeptical look, eyes dark like huckleberries. Her eyes always attract men. So do her legs. It has happened hundreds of times. They get drawn in, make a pass — usually awkwardly — and she takes it up, or lets it go by and waits for the heat to dissipate, pretending nothing has happened.

But something is wrong this time.

Usually she isn't aware of what is happening — at least not so fully aware as she is now, so aware that she seems to be acting like some wind-up doll. Her heart isn't in it. She watches herself watch him looking at her breasts and arched shoulders. She lets him look into her eyes. She says nothing. She doesn't have to. His hand moves as if he is going to cup her breast. She does not move away, instead, allows his hand to move closer to her. She looks at Jack Phillips' hand.

'You'll miss the planetarium show. There are about fifteen people in there waiting,' she says, quietly.

His eyes look away from hers. He slowly withdraws his hand.

Without speaking to her again, he fills his plastic jug and walks across the yard to the planetarium, leaving Gloria to imagine: talk, drinks, dinner, sex back here in his office on his leather couch before he goes home to his third wife.

Usually she would not have such thoughts. Usually she would not turn a man like him away. But now it is as easy as it is meaningless — to see the whole thing. Meaningless because they all end, those sex affairs. So why start one up knowing it will end because it is grounded solely upon appetite? So he's a jerk. He would have been all right. Exercise. So would the tall guy earlier with the video camera who took close-ups of her costume fringe, making her tingle as the lens moved inches away from her flesh, caressing her neck and arms. He would have been all right. She can tell that much after fifteen seconds usually.

But it leaves her so awfully empty afterwards.

So, when she can't stand it any longer, she finds someone else who makes her forget. That ends and she is alone again until she can't stand it any longer. But it's not the same with Tromone.

She touches her arm.

Her hand does not feel like her own hand.

Tromone, you bastard! Leave me be! I said I'd wait.

There is something about Tromone that she doesn't understand. She wants to wait for him.

She wants to wait.

Until now she has waited until someone else appears or until she can't stand it any longer so she goes in search of someone else. Now it is different. Something is wrong. She is waiting especially for him because she wants to wait for him, only him.

It isn't his fault. She is doing the waiting. She has decided to wait. She doesn't understand why. She doesn't even know him well enough to say that she is in love with him. But she is. Impulse may have brought them together, but it has changed into love. And her heart is firm. Her will is solid.

Now, the hand on her arm is her own again.

Tromone has left for now. But he will come back to her. He will return. He better come back to her, that son of a bitch.

*

The children.

Where were my children?

I was refreshed and felt, somehow, physically lighter than before. Awake, relieved of a burden of some sort. I no longer felt the heavy pressure on my chest.

On my way down the back stairs to the kitchen, I heard Lee Ann with the boys. It sounded as if they were coloring eggs. I had barely spoken to the boys since we arrived, but my urge to hold them kept getting side-tracked. For the first week or ten days after leaving Arthur, I couldn't take proper care of them. I simply wasn't capable. Too self-involved to be a proper mother. Lee Ann explained it to me. She reminded me that he was my first and my only lover and said it is always painful.

I stood on the stairs and listened to them. They could wait. I decided they must wait. Lee Ann didn't mind looking after them for now. The odor of vinegar hung in the stairwell. Easter eggs. I had forgotten completely about them.

Outside the water and the sky were a bright blue and the dazzling light made my eyes ache. I looked down at the lawn from my window, down from Rapunzel's room. I don't know when I made the decision, possibly I had made it weeks before, and it was all a part of my leaving Arthur, but didn't have the courage to act until then. It doesn't matter. What does matter is that I found myself sitting at my typewriter writing to the chairman of the review committee at the university with copies to the registrar and the dean.

March 30

Dear Dr Parker,

With this letter I tender my resignation to the University of Florida's Department of Anthropology and withdraw myself as a candidate for a Doctorate in Ethnology. For personal reasons, of which you are aware, and for philosophical reasons, I can no longer in good conscience continue my study and research toward my advanced degree.

Please express for me my gratitude to all the review committee members for their indulgence over the past few years.

I realize that I may be required to return a portion of the stipend I was awarded for my field studies. If so, I trust you will inform me of any further obligation I have to the University. I am fortunate to have studied with you and remain,

Yours truly,

Nancy Meade
cc: Dean of Graduate Studies
    Registrar of the University

I addressed the envelopes and put them in the mail box. The sensation of lightness and freedom — of a burden having been lifted — increased. I do not know what my major professor's reaction will be, and it doesn't matter. That part of my life is over — the scholar's life. I hope from here on that my work will be less academic, more passionate, more imaginative.

The boys are not in the kitchen. I called them and got no answer — no one at all answered me. My father's car was not in the garage. Lee Ann's purse was not hanging on its hook next to the refrigerator.

I found the boys alone under the dock, playing. The tide was out. The *Miranda* rested on her double keel in the mud. Alan and Tom had gathered a pile of sticks and rusted metal — a chain, an anchor, a box. I climbed down the dock ladder onto the oyster–covered rocks and walked through the mud to them. I didn't start crying until I was hugging Alan.

'Why are you crying?'

Tom put on his glasses and looked at me.

'Don't ask her that,' he said.

'I'm crying because I'm scared and happy and because I love you both so very much. I'm not going back to the university. We're going to stay here for a while longer. Then we're going to find a place nearby to live. Maybe at the beach.'

They think living at the beach is a good idea.

I took their hands and led them up onto the grass.

'I don't want anything ever to happen to you. I love you.'

'We know that,' said Tom.

The boys, as if they both knew what was on my mind, stood silent and prepared themselves to be scolded. Tom took off his glasses; Alan kicked at the lawn, scuffing at it much the way his grandfather did.

'We weren't doing anything, Mom,' said Alan.

'Grandfather and Lee Ann went grocery shopping. We knew where you were if we needed you,' said Tom.

'There's a Snoopy Easter special on at five,' Alan said.

Tom touched an imaginary watch on his wrist and looked at me. 'Is it all right?'

'We want to watch it in color,' Alan said. 'Can we?'

I got a hold on myself. When I am upset, we all feel lost.

'Can I ask you something, Mom?' Tom said. 'Was my great-grandmother really crazy?'

'What makes you ask that?'

'I was just wondering. Lee Ann asked Grandfather if she was, and he didn't know for sure.'

'You know,' Alan piped in, 'Crazy-crazy.'

'I don't think she was, not exactly,' I said. 'She was eccentric, but not crazy.'

'What's that?'

'It's the way Mom is when she's talking to her imaginary girl friends,' Tom told his younger brother.

'Oh,' said Alan.

'Now wait a minute,' I said, laughing. But they were finished with that topic and wanted to be pushed on the tire swing. I told them more than they wanted to know as I pushed.

'Your great-grandmother was a remarkable woman. And the more I learn about her the more I admire her. I'll let you decide for yourselves if she was crazy or not.'

Alan sat in the center of the tire and Tom, the older, straddled the rope.

'She left home when she was twenty to study to be a doctor. Not many women did that in those days.'

'Like you? Hold my glasses, will you, Mom?'

'Sort of. I was going to be a different kind of doctor. But I'm not going to be one any more. Grandmother Phillips wanted to heal people. In a way she never stopped trying to do that. She just went about it in an odd — eccentric — way. That's all.'

The feel of Alan's small muscular back under his warm shirt made me want to hold him, to protect him.

'You're getting strong, Alan.'

'Odd how?' Tom asked, swinging around in order to face me. I pushed his small knees.

'Well, when she was in the Klondike, she got some kind of fever and believed that someone was trying to poison her. She didn't trust the other doctors there. Also, she had a dentist put a great big diamond right in the center of her front tooth. Right here. And she always painted her toenails bright red. All that was considered eccentric back then when she was a young woman my age.'

'Push harder,' Alan said.

'And when she got rich in the gold rush she came here and built this house. Your great-grandfather was with her. I never knew him. They got divorced and she never remarried. She raised my father and your great Uncle Jack by herself. That was considered eccentric back in those days. When she wasn't taking care of the boys, she ran the Fountain of Youth. You see, she thought that the Fountain of Youth was actually a Fountain of Love and that the Fountain of Love healed people. So she continued healing people her whole life.'

'Divorced like you and Daddy are?' asked Tom.

'I wish Dixie was here,' said Alan. 'He would like it here better than with Daddy.'

'No. We're not divorced. We don't live together any more. That's all.'

'Why?' Tom asked.

'Yeah, why don't you?' asked Alan.

'That's not so easy to explain. We don't. That's all. It isn't your fault. Always remember that. Both of you. Do you hear me? You didn't do anything wrong, and Daddy loves you. Remember that. The problem is between Daddy and me, and it has nothing to do with you. Okay?'

'When will I get to see him?' asked Alan.

'Soon,' I said, not knowing when. 'I don't know exactly, but I wouldn't be surprised if he comes over tomorrow. After all, it's Easter tomorrow.'

'We know that,' said Tom. 'We dyed eggs with Lee Ann.'

'I don't feel like swinging anymore,' said Alan.

He was off the tire swing first. I helped Tom climb down from the top of the tire and held him close until he began to struggle.

'Let me go, Mom.'

I let them get half-way to the house before I realized where they were going and called to them.

'Hold it, you two!'

'Oh, Mom!' whined Alan.

'We're going to walk over to the fountain. Maybe Uncle Jack will put on a show in the planetarium for you.'

Anything but more television. Besides, I knew perfectly well they would be agreeable because the snack bar sells snow cones and hot dogs. The Fountain doesn't interest them yet, but the simulated storm Uncle Jack puts on in the silver-domed planetarium does.

Uncle Jack was in his office behind the ticket booth. A stack of money was on his desk ready for deposit.

'I've got boxes of Spanish fans, and they aren't moving out of the gift shop,' he said. 'What do you think about having the girls use them as teasers. Would that work?'

'I think it would look funny for your Indian Maidens to fan themselves with anything but palm leaves,' I told him.

He wore his silver leisure suit. The zipper was pulled down to his navel. A large gold medallion on a chain rested in the mass of silver hairs on his chest. He smiled at me and rubbed his stomach.

'Will you put on a storm for us, Uncle Jack?' Tom asked, politely.

'You go on over there. I want to talk to your mother for a minute.'

He came out from behind his desk and stood close to me.

'Well,' he said. 'You haven't been here in a while. What are you? Looking for a job?'

'No. I want to drink from the Fountain.'

He burst out laughing. 'What? You mean you believe in that crap?'

'In a way I do. Yes. I believe in it the same way that my grandmother did.'

'It's nothing but well water,' he said.

'That's one way to look at it. I'd appreciate it if you'd let me get by you. I want to go out to the well house.'

'I'll go with you. This I've got to see.'

'I'd rather be alone,' I said. 'The boys would appreciate a storm, if you have time.'

'What's gotten into you, sweetness. You don't usually treat your Uncle Jack like this. What have I done to you?'

'You want to know what you've done to me?' Then, without waiting for his reply, I told him. 'You've bullied me all my life and I've been afraid of you for no reason. You're just a womanizer, Uncle Jack, a cheap womanizer. And I don't want any part of you.'

'Well, well,' he said. 'We've got a hair up our ass today, I see. You've got yourself all worked up and you want to take it out on me. Well, use your hand on yourself, if you can't stand it any longer, sweetness, because I'm stupid, but I'm not stupid enough to fuck my brother's daughter. No, I'm not.'

I didn't realize how embarrassed I was until I felt my face burning. I had no reply. There isn't anything I say to him that he doesn't twist around and make foul.

'You disgust me,' I said. 'You always have.'

'Fine,' he said. 'Now we understand each other.'

He let me pass and went back behind his desk and out his

private exit. I watched him storm across the property toward the planetarium before I continued to the well house.

It is a small building with two rows of bleachers for the tourists. As ridiculous as it may seem, I half expected that Gloria would be on duty at the well. But the place was empty. One of my uncle's Indian Maidens, who recognized me, signaled for me to draw the water myself while she finished chatting with an older couple by the statue of Ponce de Leon. I used a long-handled copper dipper and tilted my head back, letting the cool spring water run down my neck and over my blouse. I thought only briefly of Uncle Jack and know that I made my point to him. I also know that he will never admit or illustrate to me in any way that I had made my point.

The Indian Maiden entered the well house. 'You drink that stuff like it will actually do you some good.'

'I hope it will do me some good,' I said, laughing. 'Maybe it's all in your attitude.'

'We get some in here, and their eyes light up when they taste it.' The Indian Maiden took the dipper from me and had some herself. 'I always tell them I'm a hundred and twenty-seven, but don't look a day over nineteen.' She laughed. 'Of course, they believe the first part.'

The sheet metal began rumbling in the planetarium. Uncle Jack was brewing up a whopper of a storm. I entered the dome-shaped building just as he turned on the machine that makes the replica of Ponce de Leon's ship heave. I have to admit it is a good storm; lightning flashes and thunder cracks and the fans blow wind in your face. Uncle Jack excels at special effects, if not at the accurate representation of history.

After the show, I took the boys to the snack bar for snow cones.

When I asked them if they would like to know something more about their grandmother and the Fountain, Alan said, 'No. I mean, no thanks, Mom.'

'Don't forget the Snoopy special,' said Tom. 'Can we leave now?'

The house is a short walk from the Fountain.

'All right,' I said. 'Off you go to television.'

I watched them race for the house. I wanted to explain to my sons how, eccentric or not, Grandmother Phillips cherished youth and love. I wanted to try to explain, to show my boys that they can actually be healed a little if they would only believe for a time that the Fountain of Youth with its clear, cold, tasteless water is magic. Some people actually feel their problems lift for a time slightly, maybe for only five minutes — but lift nonetheless, just as I felt my own lift, ever so slightly. I want them to understand that their great-grandmother did make some people's lives a little easier to bear for a time. The fresh water spring flowing under the magnolia trees with their fleshy blooms does have the power to make some people — lots of people actually — more loving for a while, and the water helps them to go on.

But there is time for that. Then again, maybe I won't have to explain it to them. Maybe they will learn that for themselves.

Sometimes I wish that my grandmother's Fountain had true power. But maybe it is enough to hope that it has power. Maybe that is respite enough. Uncle Jack has no illusions about the Fountain of Youth, but in his way he respects it. I have no illusions either, not any more; the fountain doesn't give anything to anyone — it brings out what you have in yourself to begin with.

And so I am going to resume my own life, the one I stopped living when my mother died and I went to live with, and then marry, Arthur. He must fade. I am going to free myself from him this time. I am not angry at him; I cannot allow myself that luxury. When a vision of him occurs to me, I say to myself: 'He is across the water, he is moving away from you, always moving away.' I will not bring myself to hate him, because that keeps him with me. It is easier to let him go if I let him gradually get blurry and allow the blur to happen and not recall him to me as his sharpness begins to fade. I want to prefer to live without him, without him in bed and without him in my thoughts. It may take years for this to happen, but I want not to think of him, not to consider him at all. But most of all I don't want to hate him, to become bitter. So it will take a long time, longer probably than I am prepared for now. It's best for me if I don't see him. Best for me if I leave the house when he comes to see the boys. I want him to see the boys, but I don't want to have anything to do with him right now.

I told him not to visit on Easter Sunday. Of course, I knew he would.

For dinner I planned a roasted leg of lamb. After church the leg was still in its clear plastic shrink wrap thawing on the kitchen counter. The label read: 'Leg of Lamb — boned. New Zealand. $11.72. 4 lb. 9 oz.'

Next to it I set out three jars of marinated artichoke hearts, a bag of bread crumbs and a garlic bud. Fresh artichoke hearts would have been better, but I cut the marinade with water and baking soda. Artichokes — the vegetable for lovers, the classic aphrodisiac, that curdler of mother's milk, an aperient — whose hearts I chopped and mixed with crumbs, garlic, thyme, basil and rosemary, and stuffed in the cavity of the lamb's leg where the femur once had been.

I suppose I half suspected Arthur would show up for dinner and had told no one in the family that I was serving them for Easter dinner the gastronomical equivalent of my faded love life — a chopped aphrodisiac stuffed inside a boneless leg from the animal of redemption. I was without a man. The meal defined my state on this Easter day — symbol of my status, opposite to my desire.

I will become a free spirit — yet so much freedom still makes me sad, frightened; besides I still want love as much as I want food. And I felt more appetite for him Easter morning after church, a ravenous appetite. Even as I stood in the quiet of the kitchen I could hear him breathing in my ear — 'Cat! Cat!' — in the noise and confusion of our lovemaking. 'My pussy!' he hissed, 'Mon chat, mon minet!' And I could almost feel the warm fur growing up inside of me.

I popped the vacuum seal on the artichoke jar. I squeezed the boneless roast. 'Mon minet,' I said in a whisper. 'Cat.' Then I chopped garlic as if I were trying to exorcize some kind of spirit. I opened the lamb and cut the butcher string, soaked the hearts, mixed the garlic with the herbs and crumbs. The flame in the oven brought the temperature to 475 degrees. I chopped artichoke hearts with the large-bladed knife as if life depended on it, then stuffed the lamb and retied it with new string. Temperature down to 350 degrees. "Mon minet. Mon minet, hell!' I slammed the oven door.

We would eat in two and a half hours.

My bath did not soothe me. Not at first. But as I lay soaking in the tub a gentle wind came through the bathroom window and with it came her voice, Gloria's voice, followed by her soothing presence.

She asked me how I feel. How do you feel right now?

Warm. Relaxed. Clean. Hungry. My stomach is hollow. It hurts a little. Blue. Blue and red. It's not an ache exactly, more like a tearing, as if someone's hands got inside somehow and took a grip on my heart and pulled it. I feel his hands working inside around my ribcage all slick and wet with blood, his fingers trying to grab my heart.

And when he found it? Gloria asked. He tore it?

Yes. Someone takes ahold of my heart. He is pulling at it. Two halves. I feel cold and dark. Blue and red.

He broke it? You mean he broke your heart?

Yes. No. It didn't break. He tore it. He could never break my heart, not Arthur. I don't love him enough for that. He has torn it. I don't know how his fingers managed to scoop along my lungs and make me catch my breath. Then he grabbed it like he does a fish all slick and wild, and he tore it.

Mend, said Gloria. Mend yourself.

I continued to hear her voice while I dried myself.

When Tromone came back to me, I asked him about his

wife. At first he refused to talk about her. He needed some mending himself.

I sat at my desk and began to write down what I heard.

Her Prospero

'I don't really need to know about her,' Gloria says. 'I only thought if she is coming between us that it might help if you talk about it.'

He is dressed and clean-shaven. He wears a blue suit.

'It is over,' he says. 'Finished.'

'Don't you want to talk about it? It always helps to talk.'

He is quiet for a time. Then he says, 'I will tell you about the wings. While I was home, I walked along the coast every day and thought about you. I did. That's the truth. One morning after a heavy wind storm I came upon a large red cedar tree. A blue heron, a giant blue, had caught himself in the yoke of two branches and had strangled himself there. For some reason that bird represented me with my wings. The heron was me and I was caught by the neck. I could see it flying wild and helpless in the storm. By the time I found the bird, it was battered almost beyond recognition. In his struggle to free himself one of his wings had become separated from his body. He had battered his head so that a portion of his skull was without feathers. One of his eyes was gone. His head was a skull without feathers or eyes. It was then that I realized my marriage with Edith was finally finished — over entirely — and that I could return to you without bringing her along with me. The wings which I have been obsessed with became, suddenly, nothing but false hope, or weakness, a vague and ridiculous device for escape which I no longer need. Edith's and my love had died. Our love had been dead for a long time: I only realized it the other morning on the beach. I am ashamed for hanging on to it for so long. But then I came across it hanging in a tree, strangled — his bare head and dangling wings were horrible.

'I lifted the mangled body from the tree and buried it.'

Tromone is holding her now.

'You chose to leave her, didn't you?' Gloria asks. 'It wasn't because of me.'

'No. It wasn't because of you.'

He smiles at Gloria, and in that smile is love and honest passion.

'You do love me,' says Gloria.

'I do,' he says. 'With all my heart.'

'I believe you do,' she says.

Tromone looks at Gloria. Her eyes tell him that he needn't ask the question.

The boyishness in him returns again. 'Sweet Godiva,' says he, taking her in his arms and kissing her. 'Leda! We are not so large to hold myths for one another. Let us live with our arms about each other's backs. What strength we have's our own. Let us have no more imaginary flights.'

How to describe these two people as they prepare for bed; how to describe how he treats her as she is herself, as she is, a woman of the earth, not an object or a wisp; how or when does one love the way Gloria loves and Tromone loves; how one wants someone to speak to as Gloria's body is free to speak the truth of her heart to this man — and he to her.

'You are a flower blooming slowly,' he says to her. 'I care for you, not as for the shooting star which flashes but once and leaves behind it nothing but darkness and hot memories.'

He kisses her feet, her thighs.

'You are my orchid,' he says.

'Hush now!' she whispers, 'Let your body speak to me.'

*

The odor of roasting lamb and garlic had filled the stairwell,

the hall, and seeped into my room. I put on one of the dresses
I used to wear — white silk with a Peter Pan collar. I braided
my hair.

Lee Ann had been in the dining room before me. The table
was set and it looked vast, almost deserted without the usual
place for Arthur.

My father offered the blessing.

The candles seemed pleasantly excessive in daylight.

It was seven o'clock.

My father wore his white suit and a colorful bow tie.
Everyone, even the boys, were in a festive mood.

'You're awfully quiet,' he said to me. 'Anything wrong?'

'Too much excitement, I guess.'

He covered my hand with his. 'Well, this looks excellent.'

'Pass the mint jelly,' said Alan, standing to reach the dish.

'He'll take it all,' said Tom.

'There's plenty for all of us,' said Lee Ann, quietly. She
sounded just like a mother.

'Cheer up,' said my father admonishing me. 'It's Easter.'

'I will. It just seems so funny without Arthur. Not that I
want him here.'

'Can I have a chocolate egg now?' Tom asked.

'Finish your lamb first,' Lee Ann and I said in one voice.

'I'm superstitious. Make a wish,' she said to me.

'I don't like the stuffing,' said Alan.

'It's artichokes. They're good for you,' said Lee Ann.

'Two more bites,' I said, 'and you both can go outside.'

'Can we play in the row boat?'

'If you put on life preservers first,' said Lee Ann, looking at
me, checking. 'I'll go out with them.' She stood to follow the
boys.

'Lee Ann?'

'Oh, let her go with them, honey,' my father said. 'It's good
practice for her.'

'Daddy?'

'Well, you never know. I wouldn't mind another child.'

Suddenly I felt nineteen. I felt myself go young inside and vulnerable — a sweet feeling, not jealousy, one which did not make me feel weak or helpless, but tender, for the first time in years — tender and caring.

'I know I shouldn't ask. But are you?' I asked.

'Yes, we are. I hope you approve. She's not too young for me, is she?'

We left the table as it was and went into the living room. Lee Ann and the boys were laughing outside.

'They'll have the youngest grandmother on record,' I said. 'Of course, she's not too young. She has so much energy. I can't move. For some reason I'm bushed. I ate too much, I guess.'

'I wanted to tell you the other day, but the time didn't seem right.'

'Well, I'm happy for you. And, if it makes any difference, I do approve. I thoroughly approve. You should see yourself. You have changed so much. For the better. Not that you were so bad to begin with. I mean. . .'

The telephone rang.

'Saved by the bell,' he said.

I stood to get it, but it rang only once. 'I'll bet that was Arthur,' I said. 'I just bet it was.'

'I thought he'd be with his family.'

'I don't think so. I have the feeling that he will show up here. I half expected him to show up begging for dinner. I don't want to see him.'

'You don't have to see him.'

'No, I'll see him. It's okay.'

Nevertheless I recoiled when the door bell rang a few minutes later.

Arthur followed my father into the living room. He held one hand behind his back and, immediately, I smelled roses. He stood on the edge of the rug looking at me. He didn't seem belligerent or drunk, just hot and rumpled.

'Hello. You look . . . look young,' he said. 'Where are the kids? I came to see them. Happy Easter.'

He was sober, slimmer than I remember. He wore a gold chain on his neck — he didn't usually wear gold. There was something different about his beard — not so much of it. He seemed more muscular, not as skinny and mean-looking as he used to look. How could someone change so much in two weeks?

'I was in the neighborhood anyway,' he said.

I thought he would be drunk. And I was disappointed that he wasn't, that he looked so well, thriving in fact. It is clear to me that he can get along perfectly well without me.

'I brought Alan and Tom an Easter present.'

My father put his hand, heavily I thought, on Arthur's shoulder. 'Well, I'll leave you two alone. Stay for dessert, Arthur, if you want.'

We were alone.

'How could you just barge in like this? You could have at least called.'

'I started to, but decided just to come over.'

He brought his hand out from behind his back and offered an enormous bouquet of red roses. 'Happy Easter,' he said. 'Your favorite.'

'Arthur,' I said, exasperation overtaking anger, 'you can't just reappear and expect everything to be back to normal.'

I let him take my hand.

His skin felt good, familiar. I took the roses. I let him touch my shoulder. He moved his hand to my neck.

'Don't. Please don't.'

My eyes watered.

He stopped pulling me toward him, but he didn't take his hands away.

I shook my head. Then I began to cry. I turned away from him and cried. 'You'll find someone else. You will. I know you will. You'll find some graduate student who is madly in love with you, who thinks she understands you. You will, Arthur. I know you will.'

'But I want you to come back to me,' he said.

'No. You don't really want me. The only trouble with you is that you don't want to be alone.' I made myself stop crying. I didn't want him to use that on me. 'You know yourself better than that. You could be with anyone. You don't care who it is. You don't care. I know you. You love yourself too much.'

'What about you? What do you want?'

'Since when have you started to care about what I want?'

I found that I was stronger before him than I ever had been before. I never would have been able to say that to him before. My strength surprised him. It made him angry.

'The only thing I care about,' he said, 'is if you love me. Do you love me?'

I looked at him then. He looked away at the bunch of roses I was holding with their heads down toward the carpet. He gestured toward the flowers as if they said it better than he could himself. 'What about you? Do you love me?' I asked him.

Then we both looked away from each other and were silent. The flowers I held were foreign. They were not beautiful. I held them out to him. He wouldn't raise his hand for them. At last I said, 'No more roses, Arthur. No more.'

The last roses. I know how much he liked to give me roses. How superior it made him feel to hand me something which he knows I consider beautiful. But these were not beautiful. How many times he had handed me just such a bouquet. How many times I had accepted them and gone back to him.

I held them for a moment as if they were a shield. Then I pressed them against him.

'Here,' I said. 'No more. Don't give them to me anymore. Not ever again. They don't mean anything to me.'

'Never again?' he asked. 'Not ever, Cat?'

Now I wanted him to go away. I could not allow myself to care, not then. Even a crack in my new armor would send me back to him, tumbling back. 'I have my own life to live. You should begin to live yours.'

He started to leave. Then he said, 'Dixie has fleas. She has been biting her tail for weeks. I came home after class a couple of days ago and she was so happy to see me she wagged her tail against the furniture until it bled. She got blood all over the living room and followed me into the kitchen and got blood all over the stove. She broadcast it all over everywhere, happily wagging her tail because I was home, not knowing what she was doing.'

'Try not to be too hurt,' I said. 'You'll get over me, I'm sure you will.'

I followed him to the door.

'I'm getting over you, slowly,' I said.

Then he seemed so pitiful, holding the flowers like a rejected suitor.

'Don't you want something to eat? Take something with you. There's plenty left. I roasted a leg of lamb. I'll pack some up for you.'

He shook his head. 'I got skateboards. Give them to the boys for me.'

'Why don't you do it yourself? They're just going out in the rowboat. You might catch them. They'd like to see you. I know they would.'

'Not this time,' he said. 'Tell them I couldn't stay. I'll see them soon.'

'They ask about you. They do miss you. I'll tell them you were here. They like it here. There's so much more to do. It's like being on vacation for them. And they love Lee Ann. They just love her.'

I forgot that he didn't have any idea who Lee Ann is. He didn't ask. It doesn't matter.

We approached one another as if we were going to kiss, but before our lips met, I turned my cheek to him, and he did the same.

'Goodbye,' we both said in one voice.

His short beard was abrasive.

After he'd gone, I did not allow myself to think.

I cleared the table quickly, loaded the dishwasher, set out the dessert plates, moving efficiently, trying not to think about what I had just done. Without considering the effect, I had made a decision and acted — an impulsive decision which I didn't want to think about. I didn't want to face the effects or have regrets. It was enough to know that I had made my decision and that future meetings would be like the last one, brief and chilled.

'No more,' I said. 'No more roses.'

Under the circumstances, I decided that I had behaved rather well — polite, unemotional for the most part, distant, firm — an appropriate behavior, a mature one for a woman who has walked out on her husband. Incredibly, it was not as difficult to face him as I had imagined it would be — to freeze my heart, to lock myself up and to be cordial to him — to pretend that I no longer care.

I carried the platter into the kitchen. The grease had coagulated around the lamb scraps and artichoke stuffing. I scraped up a mouthful and chewed slowly. My tears surprised me, just as the flavors of artichoke and lamb and thyme did, when brought forth by the warmth of my mouth.

chapter 5

It was warm yesterday for such an early Easter. The boys were out in the rowboat when I went by Nancy's. I left skateboards for them. Flowers for her. She told me not to send any more flowers; and she said don't come over any more. I've had dinner in that house on Easter Day ever since we were married. I couldn't stay away. Ben didn't mind seeing me; he knows we have fought and made up before; Ben wouldn't mind us back together again, but, it is different this time. She is not well emotionally and I'm tired of caring for her. When I was on the phone to Flowers by Sylvia ordering her red roses, I felt sleepy, lethargic; it was an effort to give the delivery instructions and to tell Sylvia the numbers on my charge card. I was wasting my money, but I hadn't the will to stop myself.

I probably should have gone to my own family for Easter. My brother Max wrote and asked me to bring the wife and kids. Part of his letter recalled the only time I took Nancy and the boys to visit my old home. The boys were one and four. There wasn't room enough in the main house, so they put us up in the old Cotter place that didn't have any sash in the windows. It was May. The love bugs were flying around, coupled. The hogs ran loose snarfing in the yard below the bedroom where we slept on mattresses over the bare floor. The boys, of course, loved it. Nancy refused to visit again. To her my family was a dazed, lazy, dirty group; and they were as offended by Nancy as she was by them. Brother Max told me so at the time and he reminded me again in his letter that my mother and my aunt (the two women left in the family) didn't want me to marry the rich girl. So when Max invited us down for Easter, he was joking. A divorce is fine with them. 'Did you get rid of that sour priss yet?' Max asked. 'Let me get you a cracker girl, Arthur. A stringy animal with dirty ankles and a big brain just like yours and Apple's, but one that works right.' Max believes one with some fire and a mind that can go 'as many places as yours does without even trying' is best for me. He thinks Nancy is too tight.

Apple, my dear little kid brother; although retarded, he can make so much sense sometimes that I think he must have a heart as large as the world, and it was Apple who told me not to have kids by Nancy because 'you'll never get to know your kids, not like Daddy got to know us'. He's not as slow as we make him out to be. Half the time I think he pretends he is retarded because it's safer. Then, my mother predicted, 'you marry her; you leave us.' Max said, 'Goodbye, Brother.' They are a stubborn and a clear-headed lot, but my mother is right — I left them when I married Nancy.

Now I'm without both — I haven't the family I was born into, nor the one I was trying to build. I am now a man without a family. I did not plan this. I am not looking forward to weekend visits with the boys. I don't like this situation. The split wasn't anybody's fault, not really.

But that doesn't make it any less painful.

Especially when your kin says I told you so.

The only reason Max invited me home for Easter is because I called and told him Nancy and I had split up. Instead, I went to her house uninvited, believing she would ask me to stay as she usually did a week or ten days after one of our fights.

Still, she is safer at home. They treat her like they treated her mother who was an alcoholic as well as a drug addict (to put it nicely); they treat her like a delicate princess, which frees her to do exactly as she likes with impunity because the family is rich and she is the delicate only child; they let her dream and brood and mope about God knows what; and they take everything she does seriously whether it is sitting motionless in a chair or conversing with someone nobody else can see. She is cruel and passive and looks like cotton candy when she's charming guests in her father's house where she is safe, protected, allowed to act ingenuous.

I know I should go see the boys. But that means seeing her again so soon.

Two or three weeks more won't hurt Alan and Tom. They know I am their father. I can't go back there yet — I have lost all that. Why rub my own nose in it? Why give them the opportunity? The task at hand, the most valuable action for me is to accept the loss as quickly as I can and to set about the task of remaking myself, reshaping my soul — at the very least finding my sense of humor which I lost somewhere along the way like a top hat blown away in a high wind. That is the most worthwhile act for me.

I am a memory to them now. The last time they saw me was when I was shooting the possum under the trailer. They will hold that vision of me — an unflattering one — for ever. I'm afraid I startled them a little. Also I did some damage to the trailer which I have repaired, but the animal had rabies. When they are pregnant they don't seek out people. That animal had to be seriously rabid to seek out our trailer — it had to have been crazed to come to us.

I have had new yellow siding put on, windows with built-in screens and a heat pump installed. Also I bought a new couch and had simulated wood wall paper hung in the main room. And I have it to myself. My bachelor pad. My den.

I am not devastated by this — I must admit that to myself — if anything, I feel sad, but I also am relieved as if a dull pain, one I have become accustomed to, has ceased. The world seems rather new, light, an encouraging place.

She called our marriage 'a sham'. Quite possibly she was correct. I replied, 'You seem at times to have no soul and to be interested only in material things.' That is the criticism she absorbed like a punch in the belly.

When love is gone, most couples fight over money. Nancy and I seldom argued about money because she has so much more of it than I do. We lived according to my means, not hers, which may have been a mistake. Still I have lost nothing material by losing her, and nor has she in this. I did not allow her affluence to infect our lives. That may have been my mistake.

But I like the way I live.

I always have.

And it is certainly quiet for a change with only Dixie, the dog, and me. And it's going to be just the dog and me for some time. The television's gone. I keep finding their stuff — Lego pieces, socks, hair clips, underwear so small it breaks my heart. Whenever I fill up one box I send it over to her and start filling up another one. No doubt she is offended by these boxes arriving at her doorstep like washed-up cargo from a shipwreck, but she and the boys have jumped ship; what use do I have of their lives' ballast.

Besides, it reminds me of them. This is the only place we have lived, our only home. Both the boys were raised here. I've lived here for as long as I've known Nancy. When we were still students we rented this place from Mrs McCloud. Then she moved into an RV so she could travel a little and we bought it from her. Then came the boys. When I got tenure at the university, Nancy started talking house-hunting and a better neighborhood. So I added the Florida room — a screened-in porch overlooking the pond — and moved the telephone and our bed out there. The room is bug-proof and you get the animal sounds at night from the pine woods and the pond, which I enjoy.

It wasn't until they were gone that I realized how much room a wife and two kids take up. The Florida room makes this place huge without their stuff lying around. I've got real elbow room now, real space of my own. Also it is very quiet and the other night when I opened her closet a shower cap and robe that was hanging on the door hook gave me quite a start. I threw them in the UPS box with Alan's underwear and the Lego gear I stepped on.

April 13

A woman told me once that each time her life seemed to reach a plateau or a temporary testing place she tried not to give in to panic because of the stillness, the inactivity, the groundlessness below, but to use the temporary stability as a foundation to launch the next phase. 'We cause life to unfold before us', was her message of free will. She was not saying as the determinists do: 'Life unfolds.' I haven't decided whether hers is a fatalistic vision after all, but tend to believe that all statements of that kind define a state or condition which has very little to do with free will.

Free will or not, a month ago on the way home through the pines, back from the 'cooling-off' walk I took after I blasted the trailer, I believed that I could predict with accuracy the evening ahead — the fight with Nancy would continue — then and every day for the rest of my life. When I got back to the trailer and found them packed up and gone, the bottom of my life dropped out and living became interesting once again.

What a horrible thing to say.

I was at one of those plateaus when all about one is still, and there is no ground below. Even today — almost a month after she left here — I have no idea what is going to happen next, from now on, not next year, next week, not in the next minute. At times I feel as if I am standing on a piece of thick plexi-glass and looking down into a swirling maelstrom. I have descended into that maelstrom which Poe describes and may do so again — for now I am groundless above it trying to avoid looking down. This can be either exhilarating or frightening or both — a reason to panic or a fit foundation for a new launch on life. Frankly, I have been too caught up in day-to-day living to determine whether the vulnerability I feel is caused by a heightened awareness of my own free will or of the terrifying consequences of a possible fall. I guess it is the former, for I do not feel my life is in the hands of anyone in particular just now.

All this is to say, at this moment I don't feel particularly upset about Nancy leaving me. She wanted to go back to the safety of her family, but lacked courage. Certainly, I do miss the children. I only hope the few years they had with me, the time I give them from now on, and our relationship as they become young men will be strong.

With Nancy, I followed a path which ended. Now I must find another path — a new causal chain. I did not anticipate that my path with Nancy would last almost nine years and would result in two boys whom I love. Nor did she. We met by accident. We started something because we were attracted to each other. We didn't realize the danger. When I met her I didn't realize that when you meet someone in a neutral territory which is equally familiar to both of you such as an airport or at a mall or at a public rather than a private beach, you best be cautious of the people there and observant and critical because you don't have a lot of clues to go by. Everyone dresses so much alike and affects the same mannerisms in public. You can guess fairly accurately about the guy in the dark suit and the short-haired woman with a beer belly, but the pretty young women taken out of their particular social and family contexts and placed on a public beach all look the same. I sometimes wish that I had made no commitment of any kind to Nancy before she attended a real Meade family outing with me — one of our fish fries or our Thanksgiving dinners or something ritualistic we do like putting up Mother's strawberries before they rot. And the same goes for me with her family.

She and I do come from entirely different worlds, but were too much in love to recognize the vast difference even when we were faced with it. The difference isn't the old cowman and the sheepherder difference, and not the rich woman and the poor man difference. Those kinds of differences you can handle. Our difference is the what-she-sees-as-illusion-and-reality and what I see. We don't believe the same things are real. Having the boys brought that difference between us to the surface. She wants them her way. I want them to be real in my way.

I am from a down-to-earth family. You'd call us a Cracker family — some people might call us Rednecks — a Florida Cracker Family. I was raised in Cedar Key, a port town on the coast of the Gulf of Mexico. We never had anything like the money my wife's family has, but what we did have came from cedar trees we sold to the local pencil company. When the trees were cut off my father worked for the railroad. That closed down in the forties, right after the war, so my father drove a truck on short hauls until it wouldn't run any more. He didn't have the credit line to get another truck, so he started making shine with T.W. Brewer, the justice of the peace, and they formed their own company — Brewer & Meade — and drank themselves to death. We still have thirty acres in Sumner that's not good for anything now except hunting since the turpentine business has gone bust.

We have made do all our lives and have always been content, if not surprised, with what we have earned. We were never really poor when I was young; we were like all Cracker families in that we didn't have a lot of toys you could point to, but we got on fine enough. If something broke, it got patched. I don't recall feeling that I was deprived, maybe hungry sometimes — hungry for what could be mine if I just stretched for it — but I have never been desperate for anything up to now.

It's my children that I want most now. I have to admit that. I want to give them a taste of my life the way my father showed me what he loved best, which was hunting over in Gulf Hammock, even though it was illegal, and fishing for game fish, tuna and dolphin and wahoo. When I was seventeen my father made me sign on with a crew of sponge divers out of Tarpon Springs. For three months I was with a Greek crew aboard the *Venizelos* and earned enough to pay for my first year at the University of Florida in Gainesville. It was my father's way of testing me to see if I wanted to go to college bad enough to make it through. My boys will have no such test; their way will be paid into Exeter followed by Yale. I realize they are fortunate youngsters. But what they have and what they'll get simply is not everything of value.

When I think about it now, I was fortunate, too. I didn't go to high school with any plan, certainly not of being class valedictorian and winding up here teaching comparative literature. I wasn't raised by my family telling me that I had to have a doctorate from Princeton or I wasn't worthy of the family name. I wasn't pressured into this and there isn't any way of explaining how I went where I went or why I continue to do as well as I am, except to say that I never did anything in my life unless it interested me and I was hungry to do well at it — I never hunt only for pleasure, never fish just for the sport, never love only from loneliness. Also, my arm has got to be just a little bit longer than most and my grip a little harder to break, like a pit bull's.

I cannot remember wanting specifically to become a college professor, certainly not one of comparative literature, because I didn't know what that was until I became one. I tell each new class of mine: 'Our job this term is to compare events in the great texts of world literature, events primarily of the heart. I assign nothing in this class that is not of the most extreme urgency. You must know these texts to know what it is to be human.' Each term the excitement builds; my belief in the necessity of literature as a tool to our understanding of our own humanity mounts to sweep over the seniors, who may be bewildered now but not for long, leaving, after the tidal wave passes, usually more survivors than casualties at the conclusion of the tumultuous term. Even my introductory remarks might call to Moby Dick his sublime self asking that he rise through the floor of the classroom splintering oak and bending steel to batter apart our flimsy desks. Then quickly the mood may quiet as we see Tolstoy's volcanic passion in duet with D.H. Lawrence's wildness, making the room hum and swell with the straining passion of death and love. I enjoy my work. I believe we must learn how to be humans and must be reminded often that we are thus, as we are taught to love God and must consciously remind ourselves of his presence.

When I was a boy my goal was not to make literature indispensible, alive, relevant to students. I was not so arrogant as I am now to believe I can help anyone learn about his own humanity. My father asked me any number of times what I wanted to be. 'What are you going to make of yourself?' he would ask while the two of us — father and son content together — tramped through some favorite swamp of his, hunting for something or fishing for something or trapping for something he wanted. 'What are you going to become?' His way of asking me that made me believe that anything I could name was possible. He taught me to think big. 'What? You're sure you don't want to do this for the rest of your life? I suppose you'll get uppity on me and start a fish camp.'

Who knew? I wasn't sure. All I knew was that I had to stay on my toes, especially tramping through the swamp with my father.

School has always interested me as much as tarpon fishing, so I decided there must be two people inside of me — the one who has his head in literature is not necessarily in conflict with the other who has his feet in the Florida swamps. If I ever go bust as a teacher, I can still make a living off watermelons, cabbages, hogs, wrapping tobacco, frogs' legs, mules, vegetables, turpentine, sponges, game fish. There are a lot of ways to stay alive if you're from Cedar Key and had a father like mine. We always had ways of making money; we had to. Furthermore, I consider my Florida Cracker white-trash background an inimitable asset, one with which I will not permit myself to lose touch because I married into a rich family or because I get talked into moving into some modern high-class subdivision where the houses are off the ground built on stilts made from cypress trees cut from the same swamps where I tramped with my father as a boy.

I live in this trailer because I must stay close to my background. For the same reason, I do physical work most summers even when we don't need the money — just to keep in practice. Nancy thinks moving out of this trailer would be moving up, for me it would be stepping away — a step I will not take.

I want my sons to learn as best they can about my roots; at some time in their lives I will take them to Cedar Key to stay for a while. I will take them through the oyster canning plant where my father worked cleaning oysters and where he worked later after the plant was converted into a factory for making palmetto fiber brushes — whisks, hat and clothes brushes — until the factory closed during the second world war. For me the visits are to touch home base. I gig flounder, dig oysters, collect stone crabs. Alan is especially fond of the crab trap that has doors which swing shut when you raise it off the bottom. All my life I've fished and collected clams because I was hungry, but I do love doing it. And, in fact, I was casting for mullet on the morning I met my wife almost nine years ago.

It was sunrise that day and I was touching home base by working a casting net in the Atlantic off St Augustine the way I was taught by my father. I was chest deep and saw that just beyond the surf about twenty feet further out from me the mullet were running parallel to the shore and they were as big as my forearm. There was a slight mist on the sea. At some point, a young woman whom I didn't recognize put down her bike and waded toward me. She watched as I flung the circular net above the water. The net caught the sea wind, lifted a moment and filled, then dropped, quenching the dim fire it held from the rising sun.

During a mullet run, a dull silver sheen comes over the ocean's surface that looks like a large coin under water reflecting the sun. I cast just ahead of the shimmer. And for the first time in my life, with my future wife watching me, I brought in on one cast a full net of silver mullet — all of them one and two pounders — more than enough to fill my coolers. The net was so full, I could barely haul it in against the backwash.

Which is why I looked ashore toward the beach for help and saw and signaled to Nancy standing there watching, ready to run to me.

At my signal the girl galloped into the surf not knowing what to do next. We stood together in the chest-deep water. The closed net writhed and foamed with fish. There were so many fish.

'Plant your feet,' I told her. 'Don't fight the backwash.'

A wave broke. We hauled the net toward shore with the foam.

She staggered in the backsurge, grabbing my arm.

'Just hold your ground,' I said. 'We'll go in with the next wave.'

Both of us were drenched by a breaker.

We slowly pulled the net ashore. When we were waist deep, being nudged forward in the foam, I sent her for the coolers in my truck. We then dragged the net ashore and loaded the writhing sand-dusted mullet, splitting the catch in half and icing it. When the coolers were loaded, I realized that I had hardly looked at her.

She looked like an ordinary girl. She was pretty and healthy. There are lots of girls who look like that around here. She was eighteen. I was twenty-three. But there was definitely something between us right from the beginning.

'What are you going to do now?' she asked.

I usually sell everything I catch to one of the fish markets in town. I had fifty dollars' worth of mullet in my coolers. 'You brought me luck,' I said.

She had on light white shorts and a white blouse. Both were soaked to the point of transparency. 'Couldn't you use a ride home?' I asked.

'Please,' she said and ran to get her bike.

She got in on my side and moved over only as much as she had to, so I could squeeze in behind the wheel, and put her hand on my leg. We sat in the truck looking at each other for a moment. Then I felt suddenly that if I didn't do something very fast she would take her bike out of the truck and I would never see her again and I would have nothing to remember her by except a mess of fish and a wet blouse and her hand on my leg. So I kissed her. At first she was an ordinary girl. Shy and stiff. Then I pulled away and she came after me seeking my lips, pressing against me. It was Nancy who broke us apart for air; she had to ask me if I was married because, she said, she did not want to kiss me any more, not even in the full light of day on the beach, if I was married and she made me cross my heart and swear to God because she would not be able to stand it if I lied to her.

'So are you?'

I shook my head.

'Let's go to my house,' she said. 'Daddy plays golf Saturday morning with my uncle. There's no one home.'

All the way into town, over the Bridge of Lions, past the rock fort, by Ripley's 'Believe It or Not,' she kept her hand on my leg and her breast pushed against my arm and her legs spread around the stick shift, giving me a chance to touch her thighs briefly when I changed gears.

When we got to her house, she showed me the screened porch on the second floor. And we had three hours there on that same sleeping porch where the boys stay when they visit.

I gave her my nickname for her then, that first impulsive

time. When she makes love, cat fight noises come out of her. And there we were on a porch that was shaded by trees and she was carrying on like a hot cat in the branches. It was glorious! And I have been in love with her ever since.

After our first meeting, we had the house to ourselves every Saturday morning until just after noon when Ben came back from his golf game with Jack. Sometimes she met me at the beach at sunrise and watched me fish. If she didn't show up by about nine, I'd go to her house where she'd be waiting for me. It was terrific! I lived for those Saturday mornings.

We were married before she started school in Gainesville. Tom, my first boy, was born at the beginning of her second semester in January. So she lost a half a year of school then. She was pregnant with Alan when she graduated and waited the summer and the first semester before starting graduate school. The kids grew up while she studied.

At first the trailer was a novelty for her, so was our landlady Mrs McCloud. My own life didn't change all that much when I married Nancy. I kept teaching, the same as usual. Maybe that was a mistake on my part.

Nancy's standard of living dropped when she married me — I don't think she has ever accepted that. As well, she felt odd in school — a freshman nursing a baby misses out on dating boys, dorm parties, roommates, pizza runs. There were mothers and babies here at the trailer park, of course, always complaining that they were poor and abused and fat and hot and dumpy. She never did fit in too well with the mothers here. And soon there was Alan, my second son, the fisherman. I suppose she was let down by our family life here. But I paid no attention to her disappointment.

It was not that way at all for me. I was living better than I ever had. And something else, I had a smart, pretty wife and two great kids. As I look at it all now, in those days we were living happily ever after. I got promoted to associate professor; Nancy was accepted for graduate school. She is smart. She sailed through her course work, even though Alan was little. And Tom was a wild four-year-old. She made it all seem easy, a pleasure. The boys grew. She studied. I was moved to a tenure track in the department. She seemed so content, probably because I wanted her to be that way and ignored that she wasn't. I thought everything was fine. She became absorbed in her thesis about her grandmother. That really captivated her. She knew virtually nothing about her family before she began that thesis.

The only sign that something was going wrong — the only sign that I could see then — was her visits to interview her father and her uncle and various friends and neighbors. It seems to me now that she may have lost some scholarly objectivity, which is reasonable, considering her topic was primarily her grandmother and those surrounding her — the twin sons Ben and Jack, as well as old employees.

I didn't go with her on those 'research' trips. She seemed not to want me or the boys with her. Also, she was impulsive about taking them; she worked up to a point where she was stuck and needed more information or another interview and would abruptly leave the boys with Mrs McCloud, often without letting me know she had gone and would stay away for a week or ten days. As well, I never did know when she was coming back.

Yet she expected me to be here when she finally did show up. If I was shopping or at the library and the boys were with Mrs McCloud when she came home, instead of volunteering anything about herself, she grilled me, accused me, charged me with infidelity and child neglect.

Somehow she got it stuck in her head that the minute she disappeared I left the boys with Shirley McCloud and went hunting for other women. At first I thought she was joking or responding to some guilt she had for leaving us so precipitatly — not true — she talked herself into a certainty. 'Your randy women,' she'd call them, as if there were a trotline full of them. 'Just because I need to be with my father doesn't leave you free to sleep around.' But also, there was a vicarious side to her accusations which I found more disturbing than her jealousy itself. 'You've been a bad man,' she would say, as if this were a game, and nuzzle up to me, shoving her hands into my pockets. 'Who was he naughty with this time? And what did he do with the House Plant? He has to show me what he did to her.' Nancy had a nickname for most of my female graduate students: The Puerto Rican Firecracker, Fern the House Plant, Misty Poodle, the Storm Cloud. She called Shirley McCloud 'Bones'.

The first few times I thought it was all semi-malicious, semi-horny play. She gives most appropriate names: Sallie Walters does look like a Latin Whore with *Absolutely* No Tits; Eva Marie Jones wears tight slacks and does seem to have a pair of Lips Below the Belly; Drake Gutherie-Tull is cold as a Blue Nun.

'Who was he with this time?' she asked. 'The Sponge? Was it Little Horses?'

Her accusations passed beyond naughty, beyond vicariousness, and into some form of psychosis. . .

I do feel a certain relief now that she is gone.

May 1

'It's May Day. I want to be in love.'

That's what I said to one of my students after class this afternoon — Eugenia Morales, whom Nancy calls the Puerto Rican Firecracker, an affectionate, quick and jovial girl with a shocking whiskey voice and a teenager's body. I like to flirt with Eugenia. She flirts back.

'It's true,' I said to her. 'And I have picked you.'

'Not today, Dr Meade,' she said, suddenly as serious as a fortune teller. 'You need a friend right now. Maybe the friend will become your lover. You're still too bummed out to fall in love. And you've gotten so serious. What happened to your sense of humor?'

I told her where I thought it had gone. 'So, be my friend,' I said, realizing after I'd said it that Eugenia was right. These past days I have become charmless, without humor, without even nominal appeal, vulnerable and hurt, no more capable of a love affair than of flight.

'Don't be so hard on yourself,' she said. 'I can be your student and your lover,' she said, her eyes flashing once more with their usual mischief, 'but I can't be your student and your friend. That is too intimate.' She laughed. 'Besides, I'm afraid I might hurt you by accident. She has hurt you enough. Anyone can see that. I mean, I just might say something and it will open an unhealed wound. It would be an accident.'

'You can actually see that I'm hurting?'

'Sure. Look at your eyes. Back home I've seen people afraid of being whipped with eyes like that. Small and scared dogs have your eyes. You look like someone hit you and you're afraid someone is going to hit you again.'

'Why Ms Morales, why am I graced with such frankness?'

'Because I like you. Because you're a serious person. Because you're my favorite teacher.'

'You are beautiful when you are flattering.'

I understand Eugenia Morales. I did well in school the way she does — cutting through a cultural disadvantage. School interested me as much as anything else I did. It always has. It still does.

Mrs Noland, my ninth grade English teacher, suggested that I go to P.K. Yonge in Gainesville for my last three years of high school. That place was a challenge for me. From there my horizons got wider. I went to the university. No one in my family before or since has done that. When I was a senior ready to graduate it seemed to me that I wasn't yet finished learning. School was like a project I hadn't completed — like I had started repairing this mullet net, but there were still a few holes in it yet to close up. So I applied and got into Princeton.

Now I'm a teacher; I like most of my students.

Eugenia Morales smiled at me. She has a hot, wicked smile full of fire. 'You are,' she said, 'my favorite.'

'Why goodness. *Gracias*, Eugenia. That means something, coming from you.'

'No sweat, Professor Gringo.'

'I still don't have a love and it's still May Day.'

'I still don't want to be your (she made quotes in the air with her fingers) "friend." '

Good enough. No Eugenia Morales for me. You are still my favorite student — lover or not.

Later this afternoon I tried to call my wife and wish her happy May Day.

But she appears to have gone into a shell as far as I am concerned and will not come to the phone. Most likely she is holed up in her room — playing the old pretending-she-is-someone-else, so-not-to-see-the-self game which she plays.

Anyway I called and spoke to her father.

The conversation lately has been much the same each time we have spoken:

'How are you, Ben?'

'We're fine here. How are *you*? The boys, they wonder where you are.'

'Can one of them come to the phone?'

'Well, I think Lee Ann has Alan out in the rowboat fishing. Tom's gone down the street on that skateboard you gave him.'

'Nancy okay?'

'She's not sick.'

'That's good.'

'Is it? Say, those boys of yours are getting pretty good on those boards you brought them. You ought to see them.'

'I'd like that.'

'You take care of yourself, Arthur.'

'Well, please tell the boys I called, then. Nice to talk to you Ben.'

'I'll tell her you called again, Arthur. Now, so long.'

'Appreciate it, Ben.'
'Sure. Take care.'
Damn, it makes me sad to hear his voice.
Right now is too awkward a time to visit. I find that I miss
Ben almost as much as I miss Tom and Alan. It's possible
that he is the one I'm sad about losing and not Nancy.
I never taught him how to cast a mullet net. And without
me he won't have much reason to learn. I learned to sail that
ketch of his. The least I could have done in return is to show
him real fishing.
Not this summer.
It's too late.

Summer projects

I should do more on my Francis Ponge study (the origins and
resonances in *Soap*); work on the Max Frisch monograph for
Oxford University Press about self-identity (*'It's so if you think
it's so.' I'm Not Stiller — the many personae within the voice.*)
Ponge still baffles me.
Frisch is right near the top of my all-time favorite list. I hold
something as thin as his *Man in the Holocene* and it seems as
heavy as *Webster*'s Second. His work is powerful primarily
because of his absolute commitment to and involvement with
the idea of his protagonist.
Geiser lives by his ideas, fat–headed or not. I know this old
man called Geiser who is trying to reject his old age with
elaborate methods. He seeks what we all seek, his identity, his
own particular unique human identity; something Frisch
believes it is impossible for any of us to know because it
changes as we live in time, changes even if we do not act, even
if we hole up and stop — become as passive as my wife can
become. The self, not even the frozen self, paralyzed, can be
defined. Yet we search tirelessly, endlessly within ourselves to

146

learn who we are. The search wears us into confusion, exhaustion, death.

But there is nothing more worthwhile than that search. The only worthwhile act a man can perform is the continuous search for the definition of his soul. The search for definition causes the shaping of the soul. And we bring to our search whom we have read; lucky for us to know Shakespeare and Tolstoy and Lawrence and Faulkner and Frisch and Melville and Garcia Marquez and William James and Gaston Bachelard . . . all men who describe the condition of existence in galvanizing and human terms, whose introspection appears so natural and effortless; all men who know the search ends only at our death and not before, who know the point of our lives is that search.

The better the tools one brings to this search, the better shaped will become his soul. Be careful whom you marry; and be careful whom you read.

May 5

Talked to Nancy. If I was uncertain why she has gone to her father's, I am no longer. He is not ill; he has no prescriptions that need filling, no damn gardening that can't be done by the man, no spring cleaning the maid can't do. Her voice quavered when I asked her the real reason. She sounded sad.

'No. It isn't you. It's a family thing. I had to come here. I wanted to. I belong here.'

'Stay as long as you want,' I said. 'But, Honey, that doesn't mean you have to stay for good. Come back when you're ready. I don't want to separate.'

'Meanwhile you'll play around. How can I stay married to you, knowing you're fooling around.'

'I'm not. I've been teaching class and taking care of the dog. That's it. You want to be rid of me. What is going on? Why?'

Once I asked her if she went home so often — she was

leaving me with the kids at least once a month — to drive me away from her. That stung. She denied it with fury and was sullen at any mention of her father. This mood did not lift until I urged her to visit him. When she returned that time, she was refreshed and partly herself again.

'I don't want to get "rid" of you,' she said. 'Not like you are a piece of trash. I want to live with my family.'

I led myself into my own wounding by what I said then: 'But your family is here. Alan and Tom and Dixie and I, we are your family. Anybody else is your relative.'

'My family is here with me and, furthermore, I'm going to ask for custody of the boys. They belong with their mother.' Then she began to cry. 'They deserve a decent life, Arthur, not what you have to offer. I didn't mean to say that. It just slipped out. I'm sorry. I'm sorry.'

'I will be able to see the boys, won't I?'

The threat in my voice arrested her tears. 'Of course you can. As often as you like. Just give me a few days warning in case we have something planned with the family. . .'

The phrase 'the family' does not include her own husband.

I bet it never did, according to her. That is clear to me now. Eminently clear. I am and always have been excluded from the group. She has left because of that. As far as I know, I haven't tried to take her away from her father. I started a family of my own — well, I tried to start a family of my own, but it didn't take — not this time around.

I suspect Nancy wants a family of her own, rather a larger one which includes a male about her age, but not me. That's what she is doing, whether she knows it or not; she is looking for a man who is more suitable in her group; she continues to accuse me of having low-class women — The Hog, The Wart — to make me the blameworthy. She wants to believe I have other women, so she will have cause to leave me and not have to admit the real cause, for she cannot accept the real cause. She hasn't the courage to say I'm too low-class for her, that she is tired of her Redneck-and-the-Princess game, that she is

and always will be her Daddy's Little Girl and no one else's —
unless by some stroke of luck she meets someone who is young
and enough like Ben. That man will be the one she allows
herself to love and trust — her baby-man.

I am not he. I am the opposite of the ideal. I am the kind
whom Ben is curious about, a little wary of, not like him. She
married me in honest rebellion, but her courage has failed her.
I made her feel like a rebel. And as rebels we were happy, then
the responsibility of raising our children propelled her back to
the safety of her small town upper-class life.

Now she wants a childhood for our boys like her own, one
which does not include me. She wants her father — a quiet
man, a constant and solid man — a tree of a man; not me —
the coyote. I am not blaming her. I admire her father.

She has had her adventure, now she wants a big house with
white pillars on the front porch and a big yard for our children
to grow up to be men in, men big and clean and rich and safe
and insulated from the likes of me.

I can't remember how we ended our telephone call. I swore
at her. She hung up. I ordered roses sent over. More roses. I
wouldn't be surprised if she refuses them this time.

She has her lovely memories. Now she wants her safety.
And she will find an abstracted, dull, stable, doting man to
protect her and the boys. She is not a rebel after all. She didn't
want change in her life; she wanted adventure. And her
adventure ended with two small boys in a trailer house. Then
she got scared and wanted to go home and start over again.
That's why she left me. She's lucky. They took her back,
baggage, boys and all.

And they will let her stay until she finds a protector who
will allow her the moods and visions, who will condone her
hysteria, her vapors; who might even find a sort of antebellum
charm, a deep poetic in her manner. She may be called
educated and her ideas deemed worthy of lengthy discussion.
There's a guy like that out there somewhere.

I think she is full of bullshit. There is more greed in that girl than poetry. She is red-blooded American. She is greedy for objects, greedy for love, greedy for approval. The man she will turn to next will be a child just as she is. A baby-man. He will trout fish, golf, hunt for quail and ducks in a way that will not disgust her as my kind of fishing and hunting do. Nothing this baby-man does will disgust Nancy — for they are both happy, rich children at play. She and her new man will live behind the thick safe walls of their big big house and play within happily-happily.

And the thing of it is: they *are* safe. They *are* happy, mannered, busy — removed from life and empty as cisterns.

Their safety gives them power. They are envied. They are considered good examples. I must pretend to admire my ex-wife, or my own children who live with her will be cut out of my life. If I don't admire her ways, I will become dangerous, a threat to her safety.

May 6

She did refuse the roses. I'll give her credit for that. She told the delivery man to take them back to the flower shop and to call me and find out who else I wanted to send flowers to.

I told Sylvia of Flowers by Sylvia to deliver them to the new waitress at Scarlett's, describing her as best I could — five-ten, short blackish hair with a little red in it, dark eyes.

'She's new,' I said, 'She's been there maybe a month or six weeks. I've seen her a couple of times.'

I don't know her name.

She just popped into my mind. I hope she likes red roses, American Beauties. Sylvia put my full name on the card.

May 10

I must not become lost to myself.

I have no one but myself to rely on.

Drove to St Augustine yesterday, Sunday, hoped to catch a glimpse of the boys. Called. No answer. Went by the house. No one home. The *Miranda* was gone. They were off for a sail. That hurt. I always enjoyed our Sunday sails together out the inlet onto the Atlantic in a stiff breeze.

So, to Scarlett's for Sunday Bloody Marys.

I decided once again — after three or four — that Jeff makes the best Bloody ever. . . But that is not the half of it. The waitress actually got the roses and was quite impressed, in a sort of way. I guess she was working and the deliveryman brought them right up to her. She put them in a beer pitcher on the bar until her shift was over. On Thursday, everyone teased her about her secret admirer. When I identified myself she thanked me with some irony.

'Why did you send a strange woman forty dollars' worth of roses?' she asked, point-blank.

I told her the truth: 'I've been separated from my wife for almost two months and sent them to her by mistake. They were refused, so I sent them to you. I didn't know who else to send them to.'

We spent time talking while Jeff filled her drinks tray. This Sweet Barmaid, Gloria, sticks with me. I think of her now and she pops nicely into my mind's eye where I can actually visualize her.

What a pleasant time — to put it mildly — I had with her. She got off work early and we went to a party. She knows a lot of people in town for a new-comer. It's her job. We talked. I didn't lie to her. I told her something about Nancy and the boys. I didn't go on and on about myself and spill my whole story, and she talked a little about herself. But not right away. We both agreed that it is best not to go too far into your personal history on a first meeting, better to attempt to move forward following a common interest together. We agreed on the principle and talked about ourselves. I learned a lot about her that night.

We danced.

'I like you,' she said. 'I'm snowed by the roses, I have to admit that. But I like you anyway. I don't want to get mixed up in any vicious marriage trouble.'

'You won't.'

'And you won't disappear on me.'

'I'm not planning on it.'

She took my arm as we left the party and went to her place and got immediately into bed. Afterwards we danced to the radio. That is another interest we have in common. Though we spent the night together, I have the distinct impression that she isn't anxious to get serious about anyone, which is fine with me just now.

I guess you'd describe her as a snow bird. That's what she seems at first glance — a northerner who has slept at rest areas on her way up on the Interstate 95 after wintering in the Keys somewhere, a mysterious traveller who follows the seasons.

She is a country woman and sexy. Dark eyes and a scar on her cheek (three hairlines close together like a cat's scratch) which makes me feel protective toward her. And she does a swish-swish, one-step to rock-'n-roll, which makes her my age but you'd never guess it, and my kind of people. She is a smooth dancer — swish-swish, one-step. She is refreshing. She has a very pleasant way of moving her hips — a soft way.

Yes. Gloria is very pleasant, indeed.

I swear she could have been a snow bird and been making her way to the Tennessee hill country for early summer, a striking woman with that black-red hair, the tight jeans, dark eyes, red tank top and red-red shoes with stiletto heels. She is not a snow bird. She was raised on the same music I was — jug, tub and fiddle.

And she dances like I do, the same way to everything. The dancing gave her away. I knew she was my kind of girl by the way she danced.

Then I come to find out that she is a Confederate from

Charleston, South Carolina; her great-grandfather received a field promotion to Captain from Gen. Braxton Bragg in Chattanooga before the battle at Lookout Mountain and returned home after the war to find his house and barns destroyed. The family, like so many others, did not recover from that war; the war set them back so far that they couldn't catch up again after it was over. Gloria's father was supposed to study law, but wound up selling encyclopedias door to door, which is how he met her mother — a fiery woman with an antique shop in her living room. They married and fought and had one child before he moved across town to live by himself in a small apartment with a view of a small duck pond out of the kitchen window. Gloria was beautiful, even as a teenager, and dreamed of becoming a model, then a beauty queen and finally the wife of a wealthy and powerful senator from Delaware or Virginia. She lived with her mother surrounded by porcelain figures, fireplace tools, heavy oak cupboards and chairs with soiled upholstery, Chinese vases, Mongolian brassware, Civil War medals in glass cases, fake Tiffany lamps and boxes and boxes of mouldering books that made even the kitchen smell of mildew. And wastebaskets. Her mother collected antique wastebaskets. The house was built before electricity or indoor plumbing, and Gloria Brown was raised by kerosene light. She carried water from the pump house to the washroom off the kitchen until she was sixteen, when she packed a small suitcase and got on a bus for Miami. She was serving drinks in Miami's Flamingo Hotel when she met on a double date a United States Naval officer from Lubbock, Lt. John Gloria. That first night she wore Lt. John Gloria's white officer's jacket to bed. Before she fell asleep she ardently wished him to make her pregnant and immediately to marry her and take her away on a thrilling journey for the rest of her life from port to port to port. They made love and talked and drank and made love and made love; and she did get pregnant and he did marry her and she had a son and was an officer's wife and she drank and drank and did not make love and did not talk and drank and drank and drank. Until she had the courage to pack a small suitcase and get on a bus from Amarillo, Texas, for New Orleans, without her son, because where she was going was no place for him and was certainly no place for an officer's wife. She arrived during Mardi Gras week, got a job serving drinks, and early each morning after work brought a different man back to her one-bedroom apartment with a kitchenette above a used bookstore in the French Quarter.

While in New Orleans, Gloria stopped drinking so much because she discovered that acid made the world more like heaven. There she collected nice things for her apartment and spun herself a cocoon which excluded her past — including her son whom she barely remembered any more. She served drinks to the thirsty and had all the companionship she wanted and was for the first time in her life very very happy. Though she dropped acid only every three or four months, heaven remained inside of her and she could call up the flashes when she needed them. If the flashes of heaven did not come, she knew what to do to find them. Also she realized how dangerous New Orleans is. For the first three years she was cautious at all times. Then she was cautious only at night. Soon she became too blissed-out in her happy cocoon and forgot that the town was dangerous for a barefoot woman in an Indian print dress with a good figure and long black hair. One afternoon she was riding her bicycle back from the market and was forced to give herself at the point of a knife, forced to give to a South American what she would have given freely — if he had only talked to her, if they had danced and talked and drank a little and talked and danced a little while, just a little while. ('Why?' she had asked him, bewildered. 'Why? You don't need to do that.') He threw her bicycle over a stone wall and slapped her face. ('Don't! Don't do that!') His ring caught her flesh three times and cut deep enough to leave a scar just above her right cheek bone that now looks like the mark of an angry cat.

After her face almost healed, she sold everything in her heavenly apartment in the French Quarter, destroyed her cocoon and ran away from New Orleans, headed east to Pensacola looking for a town that had the lowest crime rate in the south — not Pensacola, not Monticello or Tallahassee — and found Hastings, Florida, the home of the potato, the watermelon and the cabbage. She arrived at the end of the melon season and teamed up with another John who owned a truck. They sold melons together in Augusta. He left her for days at a time for the women in Lake City, but always returned. He wasn't bad. She didn't mind his leaving for other women, because she didn't care all that much; it was too much trouble to care. She had — since her rape — built another cocoon inside of her where it was warm and like heaven, even without acid. She built a place inside herself where she was always safe, as long as no one disturbed her or loved her, as long as she did not get too close to anyone, as long as she stayed clear of beefy goons like the one in the white Cadillac in the silver leisure suit. It was the gold ring that frightened her. She was afraid of men wearing jagged gold rings.

She had stayed with John from Hastings through the cabbage harvest, and they planned to sell cabbages together — this time in Atlanta — the way they had sold melons together. But it was her money that drove him away, though he wouldn't admit it. When he discovered that she had more than two thousand dollars stashed away which she would not share with him no matter what the emergency — a burst radiator hose, an emergency hospital bill — he plain dumped her and her share of cabbages on the road and took off without her and, she knew, did not plan to return this time. It wasn't the money itself, she knew that, but that she had kept the money a secret from him. He would not have stolen it from her — she was a better judge of character than that — nor demanded any of it. It was the fact that she had kept it a secret from him that drove him away from her because, he told her, if she had one two-thousand dollar secret she must have other larger and deeper ones which he didn't want to have anything to do with. Of course she had no deeper secrets. She had told him everything but that, told him in bits and pieces — after they made love, while they drank — the only story she knew, in which she included even the most sordid details of her life as a bargirl in New Orleans because he enjoyed them which pleased her very much. She was delighted that her past did not repulse him, besides his was not so sweet itself — a couple of wives, a few busts for petty crimes, a string of women as long as her string of men. However, no murders and no rapes. They became close — almost fell in love — but she was afraid of being close, of letting anyone share her cocoon. So her money was her freedom; she kept her freedom a secret from him which hurt him enough to drive him away from her. She was more casual about love than he was — but was more cautious in the end. Still, at first, she did love him, loved him so much it disgusted her. Then he dumped her on the side of the road with a ton of cabbages.

She was dirty and smelly that day. It was amazing that anyone gave her a ride to town. The first night she went to Scarlett's and met a couple of women who let her stay on their boat until she found a place, her new place above the stationery store in the Spanish Quarter on Hypolita across from Scarlett's where she worked serving drinks. She had borrowed from her two thousand to get the apartment, but tips were good. She had paid herself back the loan in two weeks and now had enough to cover next month's rent and to turn the electricity on. Hot showers again! What she likes best of all about her new town is that everything she needs — grocery store, the pharmacy, work, the pretty harbor view, her new place — is all within easy walking distance.

'It isn't a bad life,' she said. 'I might even stay here for a while. Especially if I can keep a guy like you.'

She is so direct. I turn her on, she says. I make her melt inside — she told me that — and tingle as well.

'Arthur Meade,' she said, 'I want. . .'

So we stayed together this morning until the cathedral bells rang seven and it was time for her to go to work and time for me to drive two hours to Gainesville and try to teach my classes.

I am picking her up on Thursday as soon as I can get there after school — about six. She doesn't have to be back for work until Saturday night, so we'll stay at my place this time.

It is now very late Monday night.

I have three nights alone. Then comes Gloria.

PART 3

chapter 6

After supper on these long spring evenings, the family goes
shelling. Usually I stay behind for one reason or another. Last
evening I loaded the dishes into the washer and listened to my
family outside yelling over the water to one another. I went
into the living room to check for dirty glasses. The smell of
roses caught me up short. 'But Arthur's gone,' I said aloud,
before realizing that the heavy sweetness came from the
garden just off the terrace. The oarlocks in the rowboat
shrieked.

Lee Ann and Alan already stood on Bird Island — a small
spit of sand topped with marsh grass directly off the dock a
few hundred yards away — both were cheering Tom, who
looked like a plump poppy in his orange lifejacket, rowing the
little white boat back across the shallow blue inlet to pick up
his grandfather who stood on a clump of oyster shells. I waved
at my father from the terrace.

The tide was out; exposed, the white sand of Bird Island
reached far into the river. When I glanced out the window
from the kitchen, I saw the four of them, all barefoot, backs
bent, searching for shells. With the tide low, the *Miranda*'s
moorings sagged; her twin keels sank deep in mud; her hull
and rudder were exposed, indecently. The piers of the old

dock which had blown down in the hurricane of 1955, the year my grandmother died, were no more than nibs now, overgrown with oyster clumps and crud and they looked like a double line of ragged rotting teeth growing directly out of the river bottom. Yet Bird Island with its thin line of marsh grass and its bright white sand glistened in the evening light. They were a good distance away and looked like lovely colored sandpipers darting along the shoreline.

Yet I could not bring myself to join them.

I did not lunge across the shallows toward them like a wild horse to take them all in my arms and declare my love.

I did not go and become absorbed, as I so easily can become absorbed, admiring this pink one and that one with the neat spirals and whorls and that one that Lee Ann showed to me later that looks like a tiny chambered nautilus and which by all rights must hold at least all of the *little* secrets in the universe.

I did not go to them.

Furthermore, when they returned, crossing back gay and excited, laughing and banging the oars — all of them squeezed into the small boat which wobbled and shipped water at each of Tom's unsteady strokes, I realized there was no place to hide from their jubilance, their relentless cheerfulness. So I slipped out the front door as they thundered into the kitchen and soon was on my way down Water Street in the twilight headed for the fort and bayfront.

The fort looked small from a distance, diminished by the upward sloping green. At the end of Water Street the canopy of live oaks ends and the sky opens.

That night there was an unusual mist in the atmosphere and the moon was up. Its light made the sky close as if it were an inverted white mixing bowl with the moon a circle of light at the bottom.

I walked onto the open expanse of green surrounding the fort. Around the moon and surrounding me on all sides was a luminescence, a hemisphere of soft light. I sat on the grass.

The humid atmosphere reflecting the moon's light created for me an alabaster dome of protection around and above me as if I were in the center of a large delicate tent with a single opening high in the ceiling for the moon. The sides of my alabaster dome reached almost to the ground about a hundred feet away, so when I walked across the empty fort green, the dome had the appearance of moving along with me, continuing to give me the sensation that I was underneath something and protected.

As I went down Bay Street toward the plaza, the dome moved with me. I went to the Monson Dinner Theater and Motel (the *Tempest* was gone and *Streetcar Named Desire* was now billed) where Gloria lived in room twenty-six with W.B.D. Tromone, the man with the wings. However, the room was not on the ground floor as it was supposed to be, rather on the second. I climbed the stairs and knocked.

From behind the door, someone answered.

'Is Gloria there?' I asked.

'You've got the wrong room,' said a voice, a muffled male's voice.

'Mr Tromone is that you? Is W.B.D. Tromone in there?'

'No.'

'I'm looking for Gloria,' I said. 'She's staying there.'

'Not here she isn't.'

'I'm sorry to bother you,' I said.

When there was no further response from behind the door, I walked a distance away. Turning back to look at the room number again to make certain, I saw a dark muscular man with black hair like Arthur's and no shirt looking after me. I hurried down the stairs and back down Bay Street.

Now with the alabaster dome still surrounding me, I walked into the plaza and stood for a time in front of the market place where I had left Gloria the day I returned home.

The Tradewinds was where she went next. Inside the singles' lounge — a converted house — the little drinking rooms were full. A guitarist and flute player had set up in the corner of what was once the parlor. A window onto the balcony was open, and I went near it and sat on a wicker bench. A waitress took my white wine order and returned with a bowl of nuts. I had been into the Tradewinds with Arthur a few years ago, but not since. The place had changed and become more pleasant; it used to be decorated like a fishing boat with nets and floats and buoys.

No one offered to join me or buy me a drink. I was just as glad of that and would have turned down anyone except W.B.D. Tromone himself.

I got drunk alone. When I left I remember leaving a twenty on the table, and smiling faces watching me, and moonlight, and I remember also the group at the bar in the main room and the grove of red cedar trees at the edge of the fort green, and remember my relief that no one laughed because I staggered a little.

The house was quiet. I was proud that I'd made it home without being mugged or molested. The next time I go out alone I'm not going to drink so much wine. That night is vague to me.

But I did notice it was different out, I was not so drunk that I failed to notice the moonlight had become harsh, and the mist in the atmosphere had blown out to sea, and the dome of alabaster which surrounded me earlier that night, my first night out alone in years, had vanished.

chapter 7

I have spent the last two days with Gloria — Thursday until
Saturday afternoon. It is not my intent to kiss and tell —
rather to tell of kisses — here. There were lots of them in the
beginning and even more at the end.

First, it is different this time.

I don't feel I am cheating on my wife. The boys' mother
won't have me. So I am free. I have Gloria for now, if I can
accept her terms of love. Gloria is frightened about being too
close. She says I am too vulnerable now and doesn't want to
hurt me. ('My affairs usually last a year.') She has not
divorced her first husband and doesn't plan to. She has put a
time limit on our relationship. If I understand her correctly,
we have no more than a year together. Then we go our own
separate ways. ('I don't go looking for another lover right
away,' she says. 'Usually, I'm lost, then I'm lonely, then I'm
very lonely, then I'm crabby. I hadn't even reached my very
lonely phase when I wanted you.') At least she is honest about
it, also flattering, which is nice. I seem to have thrown her out
of her four-phase cycle, which is (maybe falsely) encouraging.
I like this woman. This Gloria.

And second, she is curious — not too many people are curious.

She forms her questions. You can see them coming and that gives you a micro-second to prepare a response or at least gives your mind a chance to get into the right ball park.

For example, she looked around the trailer's little living room, then asked: 'Since you make so much money, since you have status at the university, why do you choose to live here?'

Now it is easy to respond to that.

I told Gloria that I had a happy childhood and a poor one (so did she), that I don't want to remove myself from my past by living in an environment that is foreign. I don't like big houses and expansive fireplaces and kitchens as large as a two-car garage. I'm not used to such living space. I don't want it. I want my life simple. I live here because I'm comfortable.

'Come here,' she said.

But let me start at the beginning —

It's Thursday. I'm anxious to see her. It's been almost four days. I wonder if our first meeting is a fluke, just a one-night stand. So I let my Thursday afternoon class out early.

She's waiting for me. The first thing she says is: 'God, I didn't think I'd recognize you. It happened so fast the other day.'

That breaks the ice. We have two days together if we want them. We do want them. We take the long way to Gainesville and drive south to the Coquina Beach below Marineland.

It's too cold to swim, so we stand on the rocks and let the waves break over us. We embrace as a wave crashes and her breasts are firm and warm. On the drive back to Gainesville, we are caught in a thunderstorm. Gloria wants to stop at a Wendy's. We take our food and park by the road to watch the lightning in the dark.

'It's like a drive-in movie put on for us by God,' she says.

When we get home we discover that we fit. Of course everyone fits. But we don't have to try. We don't need to.

There's more to it than fitting, but we fit. That's for sure.

We both sleep late on Friday morning. I am up first and go to the grocery store. When I come home, Gloria meets me at the door with nothing on but a towel wrapped around her head. She is still wet from the shower. She is warm and smells like shampoo everywhere.

When we run out of talk we make love and then we make love before we talk. It seems that the reason we are together is to make love. I am a listener. So is Gloria. So we make love between our silences and laugh when we make love. But we are not strangers making love. We simply are not embarrassed by our silences.

'It is different with you,' she says. 'It's nice.'

It is nice. 'Yes, it is.'

Immediately after making love, I am alone. I understand with Gloria for the first time the sadness after making love — love tears. It is the sadness of returning to one's self after love. We dance to the radio once again. We are not strangers. Still we do not talk much. We eat. I introduce her to Mrs McCloud who likes Gloria and me together. We compare likes and dislikes. Raspberries, eggplant, cherries — we both like. She likes peaches, salmon, pole beans. I am not fond of pole beans. I like pork chops, brussel sprouts. She has never eaten brussel sprouts. We both have had enough cabbage to last us the rest of our lives. We both like artichokes with lemon butter.

'Where did you learn about artichokes?'

'From a man I was fond of once. My husband.'

This is the man she holds in reserve by not divorcing him, the man she uses to keep her distance — so as not to get hurt.

Then it is Saturday morning. I am up early reading as usual. Gloria sleeps, as usual, I assume. She awakes and I immediately bring her coffee. She is sleepy and comfortable and lets the warm cup settle betwen her breasts. ('This is what I like to do,' she says quietly. 'Hold my coffee here and think about the day to come.') A sense of relaxation has come over me which I have not experienced before. She knows how to make me feel good even if all she is doing is lying in bed with a sheet over her, holding her coffee cup with her eyes closed, peacefully thinking about the day spread out before her. She seems at home here — or at home with herself here — which makes me feel manly for some reason. We do not talk about this. A smile is enough. I continue to read, aware of her peacefulness. The dog is with us, but Dixie is not as demanding as usual — does not need petting as frequently, so there is no need to send her away. Dixie is imitating Gloria; Dixie too is peaceful.

Soon it is time to drive her back, she must work.

'I like you,' I say. 'I could get to like you very much.'

That's when she tells me about her rule. One year for one affair. I don't believe her when she says that it is much easier to end something when you know it is going to end anyway. Why worry about the end now?

'I have to tell you that,' she says. 'I don't want to hurt you.'

I know so little about her even now. But I do know her. She is different with me alone than she is in a bar serving drinks — I like her better alone. She is whole. She is real. I believe she is a kind and genuine person. She is a loner. When we make love, I am sure we are making love to each other, together — no one else is present for a change, no ghosts, no past loves, living or dead.

'Next Thursday then?' she asks.

I nod. We kiss. She swish-swishes around the front of the car and knocks on my window. We kiss one more time and I watch her climb the steps to her apartment above the office supply store. We wave to each other. It is different this time. I watch her door close. It is different. I do not feel relief now that she is gone. What do I feel? Alone. I am alone.

chapter 8
epilogue

Those of us who remember Jack and Ben Phillips as boys can without too much conjecture observe how Nancy's oldest boy Tom is turning out more like his grandfather (the quiet, private, lanky type) and Alan like his great uncle Jack (the explorer, basically, the stumbler, the doer). More important, both of the youngsters are fiercely loyal to their mother — just as Ben and Jack always were in different ways. Jack has never found a woman to take his mother's place — Lord knows he's tried. Brother Ben, for his first wife, latched on to a woman as much like Leellen-Kaye Phillips as he could find, and for his second one, the opposite. So, in a sense, neither Ben nor Jack ever shook off his mother, which isn't all that surprising if you consider the old lady's peculiar blend of hysterical paranoia and dynamic energy, which many of us found so endearing.

It took Jack Phillips' accident to bring all this out clearly, especially the tie between Nancy and her uncle. There was always a sort of approach-avoidance between them before. Now Nancy has taken him under her wing for what appears to be a long convalesence with no certainty of Jack's full recovery. After all, Jack is family.

Nancy has been home almost six months and has established herself with the boys in the family house. Ben and Lee

Ann got married two weeks ago and decided to leave for a cruise and live after that in Lee Ann's condo at the beach. That's best. The Water Street house has too many memories for Ben to start afresh with Lee Ann. The house puts Lee Ann at a disadvantage and she knows it. Also, she's pulling Ben away from the family business, leaving it up to Nancy.

At first we thought Nancy had gone into a shell. She didn't answer the telephone. She didn't leave the yard except maybe for a night at the Tradewinds a few times, but for all that she spent her first month here holed up in the house like she was in mourning. Lee Ann took care of the children. It was as if the house had sucked her up. Then she seemed to be over it. Her father did the same thing with Kaye-Ann dead.

Lately Jack has been coming over more and more. He was even before the accident. He likes those boys. They're the grandsons he never had. It's quite a sight when he drives up in his white Cadillac with the top down ready to pal around. The boys run out to greet him or call from the tire swing. Sometimes Jack takes them to the baseball diamond at the Cathedral school where they play ball on the empty diamond. Jack is dressed in silver — the pitcher. Tom, his glasses ablaze, is outfield looking for Alan's wild fly. At first glance the three of them look helpless — especially Jack because of the accident — then you hear the shouting and the laughter. The way Jack has come to love those boys would melt any mother's heart.

It was Alan who suggested to his great uncle that the storm in the planetarium would be more exciting with the addition of lightning bolts — real ones, Alan insisted, not strobe lights. The improvement appealed to the carnival lover in Jack. He assembled a directors' meeting to approve the expenditure. The Fountain of Youth's board of directors consists of Jack, Ben (who is now off on a year's honeymoon cruise aboard the *Miranda* to Bimini and beyond with Lee Ann) and Nancy. The boys attended the meeting ex-officio. The question was whether to install within the planetarium a static electric generator of sufficient power to cause bolts of electricity to arc across the bow of the replica of Ponce de Leon's caravelle. Jack was in favor, so were the children who refused to remain silent. In view of the boys' enthusiasm, Nancy relented. Jack was authorized $5,000 for design and execution. Alan and Tom were assigned officially as junior assistants. After a consultant from the Boston Museum of Science provided plans for a smaller version of the generator used there, the device was constructed and installed. Jack raised the admission fee by fifty cents a person and projected that the generator would be paid for in six months.

So successful was this first family project at the Fountain in many years, that Nancy found herself spending more time there than she had in her life. Her uncle was fond of the boys and gave them such jobs as raking the paths and watering the gardens and filling the bird baths, much the same tasks he had performed as a child. Nancy added a feminine touch to the place which had been missing under Jack's management. The gardens thrived. Ducks were added and allowed to run free. An alligator was installed in a fenced arena and periodically fed frozen chickens. And Jack seemed to lose years due to his contact with the children. However, his interest in younger women did not diminish.

Little is known about what happened the night of the accident except that the woman with Jack was unharmed and had the presence of mind to call the rescue unit as well as the power company to untangle Jack Phillips from a mass of wires through which a steady flow of low voltage direct current was entering his body, causing surges of what seemed to Jack at the time as pleasant convulsions. He was not physically damaged by the electricity and could function thereafter almost normally. ('It was like someone kicked him in the balls,' the young woman who had been with Jack told Nancy some days later.)

As a result of her uncle's sudden sexual docility, Nancy experienced what was apparently a complete change of heart toward him. As he threatened her less, they worked better together. Part of Jack's respect for Nancy came from her having established herself (apparently for good) in the Water Street house, thus declaring herself the matron of the family. As such she began to blossom into somewhat the same sort of woman her grandmother had been at her age (sharp–tongued, innovative, suspicious, firm-minded even when dead wrong) all of which appealed to her uncle and had the immediate effect of his suggesting that she be voted the president of the Fountain of Youth Company, Inc., becoming on paper at least his superior. In fact, Nancy has begun to follow the path of her grandmother and of her mother as the next matron in line at the Fountain, and Jack, who is more aware of the family tradition at the Fountain than anyone alive, has responded accordingly.

So it appears that Ben Phillips' daughter has found herself something to do — an occupation. Soon she will be running the Fountain herself, like her grandmother and her mother ran it before her. She is there every day now talking to the tourists telling them about how the place was started and how there never really was such a place as the Fountain of Eternal Youth, but that this place of her family's is as close to one that there is. She tempts the visitors to taste the water, just to see if they don't feel a little bit better, a little younger, rejuvenated. She is planning a little museum in memory of her grandmother — a history of the Fountain's success as a myth, how it grabbed people's dreams right from the start. And though it is way too soon to tell, it wouldn't surprise anyone if Tom takes after his grandfather and looks after his mother when she gets too old and if Alan follows his uncle running the place for her. But the boys are young. And though the Phillips family is together now, it is too early yet to tell about the boys.

But it wasn't because of Jack's fondness for the children that she began to spend more time at the Fountain. Nancy and her uncle have become partners, of a sort. Jack had wanted someone in the family to take over the place for him —

actually the whole family did, knowing that Jack can't run the Fountain for ever. He asked her to work for him almost every time they met, and Nancy complained to her father about that. It was Lee Ann, the lawyer, who came up with a solution. ('Why don't you work with him?' she asked Nancy.) She quickly drafted a capital improvement agreement which set aside a certain amount (we heard it was a hundred thousand) in a separate account from which both Jack and Nancy can draw, with approval from the full board of directors, to make improvements on the place. Jack went first, withdrawing five thousand for the planetarium idea that one of the boys put in his head. Then Nancy, who will always be the academic type, requested five thousand for archaeological research. So it was because of Lee Ann that the archaeologist Nancy knew from somewhere came onto the property and set up his tent and got to work on a series of map overlays to establish the water line of the harbor and creeks. You might say that Nancy wants him there for himself more than for his research. Anyway, she looks better than she did a few months ago. The right man at the right time does wonders for a woman's walk.

Next it will be Jack's turn for a capital improvement. It may take him a while.